Pleasurable Bargains

KATE PEARCE

ELLORA'S CAVE
ROMANTICA PUBLISHING

An Ellora's Cave Romantica Publication

www.ellorascave.com

Pleasurable Bargains

ISBN 9781419956607
ALL RIGHTS RESERVED.
Eden's Pleasure Copyright © 2005 Kate Pearce
Antonia's Bargain Copyright © 2007 Kate Pearce
Edited by Briana St. James
Cover art by Syneca

Trade paperback Publication June 2007

Content Advisory:

S – ENSUOUS
E – ROTIC
X – TREME

Ellora's Cave Publishing offers three levels of Romantica™ reading entertainment: S (S-ensuous), E (E-rotic), and X (X-treme).

The following material contains graphic sexual content meant for mature readers. This story has been rated E–rotic.

S-*ensuous* love scenes are explicit and leave nothing to the imagination.

E-*rotic* love scenes are explicit, leave nothing to the imagination, and are high in volume per the overall word count. E-rated titles might contain material that some readers find objectionable—in other words, almost anything goes, sexually. E-rated titles are the most graphic titles we carry in terms of both sexual language and descriptiveness in these works of literature.

X-*treme* titles differ from E-rated titles only in plot premise and storyline execution. Stories designated with the letter X tend to contain difficult or controversial subject matter not for the faint of heart.

Also by Kate Pearce

⁊⊙

Planet Mail

About the Author

⁊⊙

Kate Pearce was born and bred in England. She spent most of her childhood being told that having a vivid imagination would never get her anywhere. After graduating from college with an honors degree in history, she ended up working in finance and spent even more time developing her deep innner life.

After relocating with her husband and family to Northern California in 1998, Kate fulfilled her dream and finally sat down to write her first novel. She writes in a variety of romance genres, although the Regency period is definitely her favorite.

Kate welcomes comments from readers. You can find her website and email address on her author bio page at www.ellorascave.com.

Tell Us What You Think

We appreciate hearing reader opinions about our books. You can email us at Comments@EllorasCave.com.

PLEASURABLE BARGAINS

೫

EDEN'S PLEASURE

~11~

ANTONIA'S BARGAIN

~99~

EDEN'S PLEASURE

∞

Chapter One
England, 1815

ဆ

"That's it, Eden. Open your eyes. There's the girl."

I half-opened my eyes as the warmth of a man's gloved hand caressed my left breast, bringing with it an unexpected but not unwelcome tug of desire.

I gathered my scrambled thoughts and gazed up at the clear blue sky through the new budding leaves of an ancient oak tree. The last thing I remembered was flying through the air as my borrowed horse misjudged the height of a stone wall and ungraciously unseated me. I wiggled my toes and then my fingers. To my relief, apart from the bruise to my pride and a slight ache in my head, I appeared to be unscathed.

"Eden, are you in there?"

I frowned as I realized the teasing male voice was familiar and settled to the problem of which of the Harcourt twins had come to my rescue. I decided it was Lord Gideon, the elder of the two, as Gervase, the younger by ten minutes, was probably abroad with the army.

"Shame on you, Eden."

Gideon began to stroke my nipple between his finger and thumb. Heat pooled in my lower body and I pressed my thighs together to prolong the sensation.

"Shame for what, Gideon?" My voice was husky, my throat too dry. "Falling from my horse?"

Gideon smiled and continued to play with my rapidly hardening nipple. His golden hair, ruffled by the exertions of the hunt, caught the rays of the sharp spring sunshine and shone like an angelic halo.

"No, love, not for falling but for not wearing a proper corset." He pinched my nipple and I could not contain a gasp. His eyes narrowed and he continued softly. "When you did not respond to my calls, I sought to check your heartbeat and found not a modest corset but this confection of black silk and lace." He flicked the silk with his fingertip. "I ordered my groom to turn away so I could touch you as I wished."

I glanced over his scarlet-clad shoulder and saw his groom at the entrance to the glade, his back discreetly turned, holding the reins of our two horses.

I arched my back with a shiver, delivering more of my breast into Gideon's deft fingers. He seemed to understand my unspoken invitation and finished unbuttoning the front of my modest black hunting gown. Soon he had both my breasts bared. I waited, dry mouthed as he gazed down upon me. Had I changed in the five years since I'd last seen him?

After a long while when all I could hear was the distant call of the huntsman's horn and the faint yapping of the dog pack, he leaned forward. He laid one large hand palm downward on the valley between my breasts and spread his fingers until his thumb and little finger rested against my nipples.

"I was sorry to hear of your husband's death, Eden."

It took me a moment to respond, so fixed was my attention on the wondrous sensation of his fingertips stretched across my breasts.

I stared defiantly into his wicked blue eyes. "I was not. I am glad to be free again."

Gideon of all people understood the misery of my marriage to a man old enough to have been my grandfather. Indeed, he and his brother had been the main cause of it. After being discovered with the Harcourt twins at the age of eighteen in a scandalous state of undress, I'd been forced into an unwelcome marriage to protect my shattered reputation.

"And," I continued, "my husband was ill for a least a year before he finally passed away. I think it was a relief for everyone."

Gideon raised an eyebrow. "I am so glad you mentioned relief, Eden." He leaned closer and I inhaled the fresh citrus scent of his cologne. "How on earth did you manage without a man in your bed for so long?" He flexed his hand and drew my breasts closer together. "Did you bed one of the footmen?"

I managed a small laugh. "My stepdaughter, who is at least twenty years older than me and a jealous dried-up crone, kept a strict eye on my activities after my husband's death." I leaned back against the comfort of his arm, releasing the peppery scent of the bluebells crushed beneath me to mingle with my own dawning arousal.

Gideon's smile deepened. His other hand slid down the side of my leg and caught the hem of my riding habit.

"I have just remembered something else about you."

I caught my lip between my teeth as his fingers closed around my knee and headed upwards. "You liked to ride without anything between you and the horse." I held my breath as his hand dealt with my petticoats and came to rest on the naked nest of curls at the top of my legs. He gave a satisfied sigh. Without further thought, I opened my thighs at his gentle pressure. He slid his fingers around to cup and then probe my slick, wet passage.

He knelt up and leaned over me, one hand massaging my nipple between his finger and thumb and the other pressing into my mound of wet curls. With a muffled scream, I came, pushing my hips up from the ground to grind his palm harder into me.

I could scarce look at him when I finished shuddering but when I did, there was no mistaking the appreciation in his blue eyes. Gideon took my shaking hand and rested it on the front of his straining breeches. His thick cock stirred urgently against my fingers as I stroked him with my thumb.

"I think you are in need, Eden. And, as I feel in some part responsible for the debacle of your marriage, I intend to aid you."

Still shocked and deeply embarrassed by my enthusiastic response to his less than intimate touch, I allowed him to pick me up like a damsel in distress and carry me to the nearby hunting lodge. I pressed my hand to my breast and felt my rapid heartbeat and the surge of my blood.

The house seemed empty, everyone else out enjoying the pleasures of the hunt. But Gideon took care not to be seen by the servants as he found his way to my room and deposited me on the embroidered chaise lounge at the foot of my bed. Bemused, I lay back as he locked the door and then manhandled the couch around until I faced the large gilt mirror beside my bed.

I stared at my reflection as I waited for him to join me. My black hair was tousled and my cheeks bore the flush of arousal. My green eyes already held the expectation of passion. In truth, I looked better than I had in years and all because of a three-minute tryst under an oak tree. My nipples tightened as I stole another glance at Gideon and wondered what he planned to do with me next.

He sat behind me on the chaise, his long muscular legs, encased in tight buckskin breeches and shiny black top boots, on either side of me. He brought his hands around my waist and unbuttoned the front of my riding habit. I trembled like a virgin at the determined brush of his fingertips.

"Ah, Gideon, I'd almost forgotten how good it feels to be touched by a real man."

He chuckled, the rich sound vibrating against my throat. "You are definitely worth touching, my dear, I can vouch for that."

He undid all the buttons, eased my arms out of the long tight sleeves and then disposed of the dress, corset and petticoats. I lay against him clad only in a thin black silk chemise, black silk stockings and leather riding boots.

Gideon sighed as he eased my thighs apart, revealing the dark glistening curls of my mound. He still had his leather gloves on and had not removed any of his own clothing.

"Gervase and I often wondered how you would look out of those terrible clothes you used to wear—and now I have found out." His thumb rubbed over my clitoris in a soothing yet relentless rhythm and I leaned my head back onto his broad shoulder and closed my eyes.

"No, Eden, you must watch. I promised to educate you."

I forced my heavy eyes open and watched his thumb brush over my swollen clitoris back and forth, back and forth, darkening the leather of his glove with my wetness. He took my hand and kissed my fingers.

"If your stepdaughter was such a dragon, how did you cope with no man inside you during your year of mourning?" he asked, his voice silky soft. I was enjoying his attentions too much to reply and merely shrugged. He pressed my fingers down towards my mound and slid them inside me. "Is this what you did?" He moved my fingers in a circular fashion until I nodded and then he slowed his stroke. "Scarcely as big as a man's cock, are they, love?"

I shook my head and watched mesmerized as he interlaced his gloved fingers with mine and thrust them back inside. A subtle thrill of pleasure darted through me. I arched my back and felt my tight sheath caress and cling to the roughness of his leather glove. He pressed his thumb against my labia and held my gaze in the mirror.

"Still not big enough, darling. Shall I prove it to you?" He removed my soaked fingers and brought them behind me to his buckskin breeches. I could not help but gasp as I grasped the shape of his cock. It was so huge, I could scarcely get my fingers around it. My body throbbed with a sensuous welcome, opening me wider, making me wetter.

"Let me see you. Let me touch you," I pleaded but Gideon refused to be distracted.

"Later, Eden. This time, I wish only to teach and please you." He dragged my hand away from his breeches and brought it to my breast. I was pleased that despite the coolness of his tone his breathing grew harsher.

"I have to go to London tomorrow, and I would hate for you to miss what I have planned for you." His fingers returned to torment my swollen clitoris. I tensed as he unfastened his breeches and his hard wet cock rubbed against my naked buttocks. I moaned and instinctively tried to lift myself and make him slide into me. His arm tightened around my hips and he held me firmly against him.

His suddenly cold blue eyes met mine in the mirror.

"I said you were not to touch me. Do you wish to learn or shall I leave you now?"

"Don't leave me like this," I moaned as his thumb drove into me, making me squirm.

"Then be still, for I have something for you." He reached down beside the chaise and picked up his riding crop. I reclaimed his gaze in the mirror and frowned.

Holding the whip halfway down, he pressed it into my hand. "Don't pout, love. This is your present, to keep you busy and wet for me whilst I am away."

"Do you wish me to whip myself?" I shrugged. "I had enough of that during my marriage. It does not excite me."

Gideon shook his head. "Give me the whip."

I gave it back to him and he curled his hand around the leather handle. "I want you to wrap your fingers around this and then think of how my cock felt."

I did as he requested as a low burn of anticipation and excitement settled in my stomach. The whip handle was smooth and large and similar in size to Gideon. I began to see what he wished of me and took the whip back into my hand.

With murmured words of encouragement, he helped me position the handle at the entrance to my passage.

He pressed both of his thumbs against my clitoris and spread his fingers through my curls, opening me wide. I watched the tip of the whip disappear into my wetness and released my breath. There was no pain, only a smooth, thick sense of being overstretched and filled to bursting point. I paused for a heartbeat to get used to the sensation.

"Take more, now. You are wet enough."

Gideon's stark commands and unsubtle pressure on the whip handle drove it deeper and deeper. I gasped as my flesh struggled to accommodate the sudden huge influx. Gideon began to rub my clitoris with hard, remorseless strokes.

I screamed as the head of the whip touched the mouth of my womb and a wave of violent pulsating need shuddered through me. Gideon held me tightly through my prolonged climax, one hand pressed to my breast, the other manipulating both the whip handle and me.

"Do you remember how we first met, Eden?"

"Yes," I gasped as a second wave of excitement hit me. "We met in the barn at your father's estate. You and Gervase were..." I paused to find the right word. Gideon slowly rotated the handle with a subtle twist of his wrist.

When I finished writhing against him, he whispered in my ear, "Eden, Gervase and I taught you the right words. Do I need to tell them to you again?"

I gave a tiny nod and Gideon bit down hard on my neck. "Listen carefully then. This..." he thrust his groin against my buttocks until there was no mistaking his erection. "This is my cock." His left hand trailed over my straining flesh around the whip handle. "This is your pussy." He laughed low in his throat. "Your choice of word if I remember correctly, my sweet. Gervase and I would have chosen something far cruder. And what Gervase and I did in the barn was fuck all the serving maids."

I still had the grace to blush despite my exposed position and Gideon chuckled.

"You, of course, didn't fuck anything, did you, Eden? You just liked to watch us."

I couldn't dispute what he said. My curiosity as to whether the twins were hurting the girls had led me to stay and watch them rut until Gervase discovered me. When they realized I posed no threat to their amorous activities, the twins allowed me to watch as often as I wanted, often performing new tricks and positions purely for my benefit and education.

Gideon recalled me from my thoughts as he tapped the whip handle again. "Move the whip in and out, just like a real cock."

"No," I gasped, "I cannot stand any more! Please, Gideon."

"Of course you can, Eden." Gideon's voice held an inflexible note. "Let me do it for you if you are too afraid." I relinquished the whip handle completely into his control. "But, Eden, you must watch because I expect you to practice whilst I am away."

I stared at myself in the mirror as Gideon began to slide the thick whip handle in and out of my slick passage. Feelings began to build and writhe through my body and I felt Gideon's cock slide between my buttocks in time with the strokes of the whip.

I couldn't watch any longer as I came with a violence I had never known before. Gideon's hand slid from my breast to my mouth to muffle the sound of my screams. He groaned and bucked and came in a hot gush of seed on my naked back.

It took me a long time to catch my breath and for Gideon to remove the whip from my now tender passage. He met my gaze in the mirror.

"Will you promise to practice? I want to watch you come this way when I return." I managed a weak nod. His expression hardened and he caught my chin. "Just because I have reminded you that you are a passionate woman, don't think that you can try your charms on any man." He ran a hand down my back and massaged his seed into my pussy. "Don't wear anything under your gown at dinner tonight. I might want to play with you again."

He slid off the couch, buttoned his breeches and departed, leaving me reeling from the sudden exotic turn my life had taken. I got shakily to my feet and ran my hands over my flushed skin. Had the fall from my horse trapped me in some sexual dream? Some of my excitement dimmed as I realized that the man who had made me come four times in one afternoon hadn't kissed or touched me with anything of his own flesh, apart from his naked cock.

I straightened my back and gazed at my defiant face in the mirror. Gideon's father had summoned me to meet him in London in two weeks' time to discuss my future. I knew he would consider it his duty to secure a new husband for me. I tossed my head. My attendance at the hunting party had been my first act of defiance. Now I had the opportunity to enjoy myself further.

I gave myself a quick nod. I had two weeks to enjoy Gideon. I also cherished the fragile hope that he might reunite me with Gervase, his identical twin. My first love and the man who led me down a path of sexual exploration only to shatter me.

Chapter Two

ଅ

I sat at my dressing table and allowed the maid to brush out my thick black hair and pile it in a sophisticated knot of curls on the top of my head. I couldn't help but wonder what Gideon might have planned for me after dinner. There was an unaccustomed ache between my thighs and a wetness I hadn't experienced at all during my marriage.

I fastened a black jet necklace around my neck and added matching earrings. The sensible part of my mind marveled at my uninhibited excesses of the afternoon. The wild wanton part of me that I kept so well hidden cried out for more. I tried to quiet my conscience by reminding myself that I had known Gideon and Gervase for most of my life. They were but three years older than me. My widowed mother and I spent most of our summers ensconced at the Harcourts' country house where I had been allowed to share the twins' lessons and run wild with them in the confines of the estate. My mother's remarriage left me alone with the twins the summer I reached the dangerous age of eighteen.

After that, my forced marriage dragged me to the cold northern climate of Glasgow and I lost touch with my Harcourt relations. Gideon's reappearance in my life seemed destined. I nodded my approval to the maid and stood up, shaking the folds of my drab black evening gown around me.

I was a free woman for the first time in my life. I grimaced in the mirror—at least until I was pushed into another marriage. I knew in my heart that Gideon would never hurt me and I was determined to enjoy him.

I came down the stairs and met my hostess, another vague relative, Lady Georgiana Woodson. She received me in the golden luxury of the drawing room. I gazed at her pink high-waisted gown with deep envy and wished I had the funds to replace my hated black clothes.

Georgiana was newly married and considered one of the most dashing young wives of *the ton*. I had wondered why she was so insistent I attend her husband's hunting party but now guessed she had been put up to it. She gave me a conspiratorial smile as she held out her hand.

"Eden, my dear, come and meet the man who expressly ordered me to invite you to my home."

I forced myself not to smile when she towed me across the Turkish carpet towards an immaculately dressed Gideon. Gideon bowed low to me. I admired the way his dark blue coat slid over his muscled shoulders. A discreet diamond pin glinted in the snowy folds of his cravat. As he took my hand, I allowed myself one quick glance at the front of his tight biscuit-colored breeches, remembering what lay within.

I had bathed but his scent clung to my skin. I wondered if Georgiana would notice as my heart raced and my nipples tightened in anticipation at his appreciative lazy gaze.

Georgiana flitted away, apparently well pleased with her matchmaking, and left us alone. Gideon brought my gloved hand to his lips and bit down on my palm. I shivered and stepped closer. His eyes narrowed.

"So you have decided to be brave then?"

He turned me slightly away from the room, dipped his fingers inside my bodice and grazed my nipple with his thumbnail. "You must want me a lot."

I regained my breath. "I want to be touched, Gideon. In truth, after all those years with that old man, I deserve to be worshipped."

Gideon lifted his glass, toasted my show of bravado and led me towards the dining room. There were only four other young couples in the dark paneled room. Georgiana ran an informal house and I was able to slide into a chair next to Gideon.

The meal progressed at its usual gentle pace, only Gideon's presence at my elbow a distraction and a lure. He took every opportunity to touch me that was offered, opening my napkin for me and spreading it across my knees, brushing my hand as he helped me with my silverware. Soon my skin tingled and I became edgy with desire.

Georgiana dismissed the servants and dispensed with the custom of the ladies leaving the gentlemen to their port. Then, in flagrant disregard for propriety, she quit her seat to perch on her husband's knee. As the port and Spanish cigars circulated more freely, she shared her husband's port glass and kissed him quite openly on the mouth.

Gideon smiled as he observed my slightly shocked expression and murmured, "You have been away from polite society for too long, my love."

I had just begun to relax and enjoy my wine when Gideon winked at me. He moved his chair closer, slid his hand up my leg under my skirts and settled his fingers over my naked mound. I almost shrieked in a most unladylike fashion as he flicked and circled my swollen clitoris with his fingertip. I glanced wildly around the table, but nobody seemed to have noticed.

The desire to scream welled in my throat as Gideon pinned me back into my chair and slid one long finger inside me. I shot to my feet.

"Excuse me, Georgiana. I am a little...overheated." I gasped and aimed a kick at Gideon. "I think I'll take a stroll in the garden."

Georgiana waved a languid hand at me as her husband bent his head to her bared nipple and I made my escape.

The weather continued mild for spring and I paused to breathe in the sweet scent of herbs and early daffodils. Too late, I heard the dining room doors open and shut behind me and then Gideon stood by my side. I glared at him. He offered me his arm and an innocent smile and strolled with me into the shadowy green depths of the garden.

With suspicious ease, he guided me to a secluded, seductively lit arbor and gestured for me to sit on the rustic willow bench. I frowned up at him and demanded, "You seem to know your way around this garden very well. How many other women have you lured out here to seduce?"

He came down on one knee in front of me. "A few. Why, does it bother you?" He cocked his head to one side. I studied his flawless profile and gave in to an overwhelming temptation to trail my finger over his luscious, warm mouth.

"A little," I admitted as he began to fold back my skirts with practiced ease. "But then, I am scarcely your mistress, am I? And I cannot claim to be in love with you." I pretended to pout. "You haven't let me touch you or give you any pleasure."

"No," he said as he reached the apex of my thighs and pulled my legs apart. "Nor are you going to." His mouth quirked. "Consider this my gift to you and just enjoy it."

He took his gloves off and stroked me between the legs. My stomach tensed with anticipation. "God, you are wet again but, I think, a little tender. Luckily, I have just the thing to cool you down."

He withdrew his other hand from behind his back and produced a large glass dish full of lemon ice.

"You forgot your dessert."

I licked my lips as he moved to sit alongside me, leaving my skirts hiked up around my waist. He dipped his fingers into the shards of flavored ice and eyed me with great concentration.

"Your nipples look hot too, love. Lower your bodice and let me tend to them."

I hastened to obey him and pushed my bodice off my shoulders until my breasts jutted out towards him. I gasped as his fingers massaged the ice into my nipples and leaned towards him. He reapplied the ice until my nipples stood rock hard and I was beginning to pant with desire.

He took my hand and pushed my fingers inside my tight sheath as he bent forward and sucked my right nipple into his mouth. I moaned as his hot wet tongue clashed and fought the coldness of my nipple. I pushed my fingers deeper and felt the clench and release of my pleasure.

Gideon scooped up another handful of ice and crushed it against my well-sucked and warmed right nipple. Then he suckled the frozen left one. I couldn't stop coming as he repeated the process again and again.

When he paused and pushed me down onto my back, I could only gaze up at his lazy narrowed eyes with mute appeal. He smiled and balanced the half full dish of ice in between my breasts.

"Are you cooler now?"

I shook my head and his gaze lowered to between my legs. He scooped up a huge palm full of the yellow ice and pressed it into my pussy. I almost came off the seat as the exquisite coldness collided with the heat he had built within me. With a murmur of appreciation, Gideon knelt up and brought my legs over his shoulders. He used one hand to support my back while he poured the remainder of the lemon sorbet into my slick passage.

He pretended to sigh as he considered the fast melting ice. "Now, I suppose, you want me to lick it off."

"Yes." I tried not to sound too eager. My hips jerked upwards towards the tantalizing promise of his mouth.

"Ask me properly then."

I knew what he wanted me to say. He and Gervase had delighted in teaching me every filthy word in their vocabulary. They had made me use the words if I wished to see or discuss anything they had done sexually.

"Please, Gideon, I want you to lick my pussy."

His smile widened. "Ah, Eden, you remembered." He bent his head, his warm breath feathering my thighs. "Of course I will, love. Hold still now."

The next few minutes were so exquisite that I lost all sense of place and time. Gideon slowly lowered his head, his warm breath already sending sparks of anticipation through my stimulated flesh. His tongue felt rough against my icy skin as he slowly circled my clitoris. I clenched my fingers on the bench as he sucked my swollen bud into his mouth and held it there.

Still sucking, he slid one finger into my eager sheath and curled it around. The fragrance of lemon infused my senses along with the heavy scent of my own arousal. I dug my heels into Gideon's shoulders, trying to bring myself closer to his tantalizing mouth. It became difficult to breathe as his delicate rhythmic torture continued. I had to come or I would explode...

When I regained my senses, Gideon sat beside me, one hand on my bare stomach. I stared up into a darkened sky.

"Eden?" Gideon's voice was quiet. "Are you ready to come back to the house?"

I nodded and he helped me rearrange my clothing into some semblance of order although I was still sticky in places. We walked back towards the opened doors into the dining room. As we approached, Gideon laid a warning hand on the back of my neck and whispered close to my ear.

"I think Georgiana and her husband are still here. Listen." I slowed my breathing and made out the creak of a chair and the soft moans of a woman. Gideon tugged at my hand and we slipped silently into the shadowed room. Georgiana's skirts were pulled up and she straddled her husband. Her corset and bodice were undone, revealing her naked back. His hands gripped her hips, lifting and lowering her onto his cock.

I must have made a slight movement because Lord Woodson caught Gideon's eye and winked. Some unspoken message seemed to pass between them. Gideon placed my hands on the back of the chair at the opposite end of the table and lifted my skirts. His hand fumbled with the buttons of his breeches and then his cock sprang free and jabbed in between my buttocks.

Still holding Lord Woodson's heated gaze, Gideon pulled down my bodice and closed his fingers over my breasts. Lord Woodson must have whispered something in Georgiana's ear as he maneuvered her around so that she could see Gideon and me from the side. I tensed as Gideon began to thrust against my buttocks to the tempo Lord Woodson set with his wife.

"Don't pretend to be shocked, Eden," Gideon muttered. "You've always liked to watch."

He was right, damnation. I could feel my own excitement rising as I watched the others couple. Georgiana's small breast fit completely inside her husband's eager mouth as he suckled. Her hair tumbled in luxuriant waves over her shoulders as she rested her head on his shoulder.

Gideon continued to rock against me. Georgiana whimpered as Lord Woodson raised her up off his cock. He slowly pulled up her skirts and turned her until we could see her pussy poised over his shaft. Despite his wife's ecstatic cries, I noticed he wasn't as large as Gideon. He groaned as he brought her down over him in one swift movement.

Gideon brought his right hand around and plunged all four fingers inside me. Expert that he was, he tempered his strokes until Georgiana started to come. A moment later, he allowed us both to find our release.

Before I had scarce finished shuddering, Gideon picked me up and almost ran up the stairs with me to my bedroom. He was panting hard as he dropped me on the bed. I fought against his efforts to release me as I felt his dripping cock graze my thigh. I tried to pull him against me. In desperation, I moaned.

"Please, Gideon, I want you so badly. I mean I want your cock inside me. Please."

His expression changed and he pushed me back against the pillows.

"No. Think of me as just a pleasure giver. Not a pleasure seeker."

He buttoned his breeches over his still-hard cock with an obvious effort. "If you can't accept this, tell me now and I will not return from London at all."

I gazed up at his determined face and thought about the sexual delights I had experienced in the past day. Was I stupid enough to stop him when I faced another loveless marriage? No, I was far too selfish. I needed him.

"I am sorry, Gideon." I reached for his hand. "I promise that your virtue will be safe with me." His expression relaxed into his normal lazy smile.

"Good." He leaned over me and kissed my fingers. "For I have never had such an adept and willing pupil." He flicked my cheek. "I will bring you some pretty clothes from London, if you permit."

I nodded. Trust Gideon to know what I craved. He headed for the door and then turned.

"I have already spoken to Georgiana. She will arrange for you to be escorted to my house in Wanstead. It is more secluded and yet closer to London for when you have to go and meet with my father. Georgiana will pretend that you are still with her, should anyone inquire."

It wasn't until I extinguished the lights and lay my sorely overexcited body down to rest that I wondered how Gideon knew I had to meet his father. Too sleepy to care, I shut my eyes, tucked my hand between my legs and began to relive my amorous adventures.

Chapter Three

೫

Two days later, as promised, I found myself ensconced in a luxurious bedchamber in Gideon's house in rural Wanstead. Pale silver draperies complemented delicate French furniture and gray silk covered walls. Despite the beauty, I paced nervously as I heard the sound of his boots ringing on the marble staircase.

I resisted the temptation to fly into his arms. Gideon was the more fastidious of the twins, while Gervase was the one who loved to touch and be touched.

While alone at Gideon's house, my thoughts turned increasingly to his twin brother, Gervase. It was he who had first discovered me watching Gideon make love to one of the dairymaids. I still remembered the flush of rage on his cheeks as he laid me over his knee and began to spank me. His anger turned to amusement when I turned my head in his lap and nuzzled his groin. My delight as he had sworn and got hard for me surprised and intrigued him as did my many frank questions.

In my room there was a portrait of the twins painted when they turned eighteen. I had spent most of the last two days studying it. The artist depicted the twins in profile, facing each other like a golden two-headed coin. Even at eighteen, I could see the differences in them which, if Gideon was anything to go by, had but accentuated over the intervening years. Gideon's face lacked the decision of Gervase's and he seemed to hide his true self under his lazy smile. Gervase stared boldly at his twin, a challenge in his eyes.

I turned my gaze from the portrait as Gideon came through the door and bowed exquisitely. A footman trailed behind him and deposited a plethora of boxes marked with a famous modiste's name on my silk-canopied bed. I squealed with delight and headed towards them. Gideon caught my arm, his eyes full of amusement.

"Not yet. You have to earn them. I've been thinking about you coming for me for three days flat now and I can't wait another moment."

I gave a shrug and an exaggerated sigh and led Gideon to the couch opposite the large gilded mirror on the wall.

"Take everything off, slowly. I want to enjoy it." Gideon commanded and I was happy enough to oblige. I slipped out of my clothes until I was naked except for my stockings. Gideon didn't take his eyes from me as he opened his breeches and began to caress his cock.

"Come here." His voice was guttural as I walked slowly towards him. "Put one foot up on the couch." I obeyed and his fingers slid in between my legs. I half closed my eyes and looked down at his straining cock, which seemed to grow bigger by the second.

"Christ, you are absolutely soaking and I haven't even touched you yet." He brought his fingers forward and showed me how wet they were then massaged the creamy fluid into his cock. "Show me how you come with my whip inside you."

I smiled and took my time driving the whip handle in and out of me until I peaked and came with a satisfying rush of excitement. I caught Gideon's gaze in the mirror as I realized that he hadn't yet come.

"That was very nice, Eden, but I think that you need to stretch a little more." He took control of the whip and pushed it back inside me. I struggled to watch as, with an abrupt flick of his wrists, he circled the whip handle with both hands and drove his two longest fingers down the sides of the handle and thus inside me, stretching me even wider. He began to pump his hands up and down, his thumbs pressed hard on my clitoris, more fingers holding the whip and plunging inside of me until both his hands encircled the width.

I screamed as my sheath tightened and clenched and waves of pleasure crashed over me. I gulped in a breath, fearing I might lose consciousness. Mercifully he stopped moving the whip. I looked in the mirror and gasped at how wide he had made me. I moved a fraction and another shudder ran through me. Gideon exhaled and removed his hands. I whimpered at the loss and strove to pull his hand back.

Instead, he gripped his shaft and pumped hard until he came with a sudden jerking stream of come. He removed the whip and studied my dripping pussy. I bit my lip as he circled my labia with his finger.

"It's all right, love. I'll give you something to ease the emptiness. Hold still." He withdrew a large linen handkerchief from his pocket and cleaned his seed and my wetness from between my legs and buttocks. His handkerchief was soaked by the time he finished. I watched in fascination as he twisted the fabric around and fashioned it into a fair approximation of a cock. I shivered as he pushed the knotted, wadded fabric deep inside me.

"Does that help a little?" I nodded and he took my hand and led me to the bed. "I have some business to attend to this afternoon. I suggest you sleep and I will see you at dinner." I could do no more than manage another weak nod in his direction as he headed downstairs. I curled up in a ball, forcing the handkerchief to remain in my still sensitive passage. Delicious shudders continued to torment my breasts and womb as I obligingly fell asleep.

Dinner was served in the smaller of the two dining rooms. Gideon had dismissed his staff so we ate alone without ceremony. Even so, the table could have seated eight and I felt a little overwhelmed. The dark crimson décor and portraits of Harcourt ancestors glowering down at me did little to increase my appetite. Gideon, normally the perfect host, seemed ill at ease, his attention on the clock or on the door. My efforts at conversation soon petered out. By the time we reached dessert I had given up.

I was not completely surprised when, sometime after nine, I heard a familiar if harsher voice ring out in the hallway.

"Gideon, where in hell's name are you? After leaving me desperate messages around half of London you should at least have the courtesy to be on your deathbed."

My gaze flew to the door where Gervase, Gideon's twin, stood framed in the doorway. He hadn't bothered to shed his cloak or his gloves and his guinea gold hair had curled in the rain. His face was harder than Gideon's and his stance more rigid. I glimpsed the muted sheen of his scarlet and gold dress uniform under his muddy cloak. His narrowed blue eyes flew past Gideon and settled on me. I stiffened at the arctic blast of his furious gaze.

He stripped off his gloves as he advanced down the room, his attention on Gideon who displayed no visible alarm. "Georgiana told me that you had a new mistress." He flicked a contemptuous glance in my direction, "Is that why you sent for me, to gloat?"

Before Gideon could speak, I leapt to my feet and came around the table to stand toe to toe with Gervase. I had to lift my chin to see into his eyes. Why did he suddenly seem so much taller and more threatening than Gideon?

"For your information, Gervase Harcourt, I am not your brother's mistress." My anger died a little at his skeptical stare. I forced myself to continue. "If you wish to inquire into what is a private matter between your brother and me, then I cannot stop you. I do not, however, have to stand here and listen to you malign me."

With a toss of my head I attempted to step around him. He caught my elbow and yanked me close.

"I was your first lover, Eden. Doesn't that give me any rights?"

31

His voice was deeper and harder than I remembered. The compelling charm underscored by the harsh tones of command. His arm muscles flexed under his coat as he easily fought off my attempts to escape him.

I cast a quick glance over my shoulder at Gideon who looked unsurprised at this revelation. A vague foreboding came over me as I took in Gideon's smug expression.

"You brought me here for Gervase, didn't you?" I whispered. Gideon bowed his head in acknowledgment. "You wanted him to find me."

Full of indignation, I again tried to slip free of Gervase's unyielding fingers.

"Your rights, as you call them, Gervase, ended when you went off to London and left me to the mercy of your father and a hasty marriage." I knew my voice was trembling but I could do nothing to control it. "What I choose to do with your brother in recompense for eight years of hell has nothing to do with you."

Gervase retained his grip as he shrugged out of his cloak. "Hell, Eden? You know damn well why I left," he roared. "You told me to!"

Gideon cleared his throat and brought a glass of brandy around the table to give to Gervase who continued to glare at me.

"Gervase," he said softly, "Father recently told me why Eden asked you to leave. Will you allow me to…"

Gervase shook his head, his expression menacing. "No, Gideon, let the black widow explain."

My indignation rose to new heights at his stubborn male perversity. "I told you to leave because your father informed me you were already betrothed and that if I kicked up a fuss he would disinherit you."

Gervase dropped his hand from my arm. I was at last able to stumble towards the door. My eyes filled with tears as I realized anew what I had been forced to give up. No wonder I had allowed Gideon to touch me. He was as close as I could get to Gervase.

"Eden, wait."

It was Gideon who barred my way this time. "Gervase and I didn't know what my father threatened. Gervase was told that you had chosen to marry a man who was wealthier than he was." Gideon stroked my cheek. "I have gone to great lengths to bring you together. You used to be such good friends. At least stay and talk to him."

I managed a nod and Gideon left, blowing us both a kiss over his shoulder. I turned back to the dining table. Gervase slumped in a chair, nursing the brandy Gideon had given him, one hand clenched in his hair. I took a step towards him, the swish of my silk skirts loud against the silence and the rain, which brushed the window panes.

Gervase lifted his head, his blue eyes full of the echoes of past pain. "I was never betrothed, Eden. My father lied to you. I am not that much of a bastard. I left because you told me to."

I regarded him steadily, my hands twisted together on the bodice of my dress. "And I did not forsake you for a wealthier man."

Our gazes locked, clung and his expression softened. Gervase raised his glass and toasted me.

"Well then, shall we agree that we were both too young and too easy for my father to manipulate?"

I took another step forward and then another. As I drew near, his hand shot out, curled around my waist and pulled me into his lap. With a sigh, I rested my cheek on the gold braid of his jacket. He groaned and bit my neck. I breathed in a waft of brandy and the hint of rain from his skin.

"Can we be friends again then, Gervase?" I asked, lifting my eyes to his and flinching at the rising frustration I saw there. He buried his hand deep in my hair.

"No," he growled. "Not friends. I have wanted to touch you like this for years, Eden." He bit a little harder. "I've spent more nights than I care to count dreaming of you lying beneath that old man. And too many mornings waking up hard and desperate to come for you."

I gasped as his hand slid up from my waist and brushed the underside of my breasts.

"You had nothing to fear, Gervase. My husband barely touched me. I thought only of you when he did." I shuddered at the memory. "It was the only way I could stop myself from screaming."

With a snarl, Gervase lifted me from his lap and swept the table clear. A cascade of fine crystal and china hit the floor with a crash. Thankfully nobody came running. He laid me down on the tablecloth and I opened my legs to him as he fumbled with his breeches. I had but a moment to catch my breath before he was on top of me, his engorged cock pushing at my entrance.

He planted his hands on either side of my head, arched his back and drove into me with all his power. I caught my breath as his hard length settled deep inside my welcoming body. Thank goodness I'd removed the handkerchief. His first full thrust pushed me halfway across the table.

"Take more, Eden. I need you to take it all."

I managed to open my eyes at Gervase's guttural demand and looked down. If Gideon had sought to prepare me for Gervase, he had vastly underestimated his brother's size. A good three inches of Gervase's cock still begged entrance into my beleaguered body. God, but I wanted to take every bit inside of me.

I shut my eyes and lifted my hips off the table. With a triumphant shout, Gervase surged forward. His tongue thrust into my mouth in the same eager pattern as his cock. He allowed me no time to get used to his massive presence but began to drive into me with all his strength. I thrust back at him, eager to experience every second of desire, desperate for the smack of his flesh against mine.

He didn't slow his pace, each hard stroke of his cock bringing mindless pleasure and spiraling delight. My sheath tightened and tightened until I screamed with the intensity of it. I came so hard, milking his shaft, holding him deep within me that I tried to buck him off. He groaned and pressed me down onto the table.

He waited until I finished pulsating around him and then drew back one last time. He captured my face between his hands, not a hint of apology on his face for his rough treatment.

"This time must be for possession. The next will be for your pleasure."

He thrust forward again. My body urged him on, quickening again with his fierce intensity, igniting a sensual frenzy until I felt the hot welcome spurt of his seed deep inside me. He collapsed heavily onto my breast until his breathing began to even out.

Without ceremony, he picked me up, his cock still inside me. I wrapped my arms and legs around him and clung on. There was no one in the hall as he carried me towards the stairs. I felt him jabbing up inside me and I began to feel warm again. We were only halfway up the grand staircase when he grew even larger and every jolting step became a shaft of mingled pleasure and frustration.

My fingers bit into his shoulders, urging him to look at me, wanting him to stop. On the verge of coming, I managed to gasp his name.

"Gervase..."

He took one look at my pleading face and paused to turn my back to the oak-paneled stair wall. When he had me firmly wedged against the wall he removed his hands from my body and placed them on either side of my head. With a grunt, he straightened his legs and thrust upwards. My body crashed down to meet him, all my weight held and centered on his now engorged shaft. It was the most incredible sensation. I strained to meet every thrust until control left me and I moaned in ecstasy.

Without bothering to speak, Gervase picked me up again and carried me to my bedroom. He tossed me onto the bed and began to undress, his eyes intent on me, his cock rampant. He sat on the side of the bed and stripped off my clothes.

When I was naked, he pulled me to my feet and made me stand in between his thighs. I stared boldly back at him, drinking in the hard muscular lines of his body and the strength of his desire evident in his wet, dripping cock. In awe, I fell to my knees and opened my mouth to taste him. He groaned as I licked the drops of pearly fluid from the tip of his shaft and inserted my tongue into the wet purple slit.

He grasped my waist, lifted me and twisted me around until I crouched over him on the bed, my mouth still surrounding the head of his cock. He ran his fingers around the join between my mouth and the straining fullness of his erection.

"Please, Eden…"

With a purr of pleasure, I slid my tongue up and down, taking as much of him into my mouth as I could and caressing the rest with my fingers. He groaned in time with my skillful mouth and grew and grew until I feared I might choke. I stopped thinking as he filled my mouth and his hips thrust forward in helpless response. I almost lost my rhythm as he pulled me astride his face and began to torment my swollen pussy with his tongue and teeth.

I sucked harder and faster as his excitement increased. I lost myself in the textures of his body and the roughness of his cock thrusting against the roof of my mouth.

"Damnation," Gervase swore. "I'm going to come if you keep this up. Do you want that?"

I kept on until he surged into me with a mighty roar. I kept sucking as a stream of his seed pumped down my throat. He rolled away from me and buried his head in his hands.

"Christ, Eden, I wanted this time to be for you." I smiled and licked my lips. The frustration disappeared from his face. He knelt up on the bed and faced me, hands on hips. He glanced down at his cock, which was already filling out again, and groaned. "I don't know what you do to me but I've never been this hard for so long or recovered so quickly."

I collapsed back against the pillows, legs open, and just looked at him. One of his eyebrows arched. "Ah, so I have to pay for my pleasure by pleasuring you?" I nodded and began to play with one of my nipples. He moved and within an instant crouched over me, his fingers taking over the caress.

"I wanted it to be slow this time. I wanted it to be like the first time. Do you remember, love?" Gervase brushed a kiss over my mouth. "I spent a whole day touching you until you were able to accept my cock inside you." He looked down as his cock stirred as if in memory and thrust upwards toward his waist. "Of course, I wasn't quite this big all those years ago or I doubt I would've fitted you were so tight."

I stirred at the memory of that voluptuous afternoon of my eighteenth birthday when Gervase had introduced me to sex without Gideon's knowledge. It had been his birthday present to me and had, of course, ruined me for any other man.

I reached out a languid hand and grasped his cock, enjoying the slick wetness and the hardness within.

"I am glad that you didn't show me this before you took my virginity. I would have run away screaming, convinced it wouldn't fit."

Gervase grinned and removed my hand, making him look surprisingly like Gideon. "No, stop playing with me, it is your turn now. What would you like? My fingers, my mouth, all of me?"

"Yes," I murmured, closing my eyes. "Surprise me."

"Eden..." his voice held a warning note. "Open your eyes. I like to watch you come."

I opened my eyes and found him kneeling in front of me, his cock hard and ready. He watched me stare at his cock and his expression changed. "Come here..." his voice roughened as his grabbed me around the waist and pulled me down hard onto his engorged shaft. I caught his shoulders for support as he began to move hard and fast. "I can't be slow, damn you, when you look at me like that, I can't."

I didn't care as he brought me expertly to climax then slid out of me. He turned me onto my stomach and arranged me on the edge of the bed. He spread my legs wide with impatient hands and stood behind me. He grasped my hips and jerked me back against him as he drove forward. We both groaned at the impact of flesh on flesh.

He withdrew and did it again and again until I thought the heat from my body would set fire to the sheets. Then, when my throat hurt from the screams I stifled in the bedclothes, he brought one of his hands around to torment my clitoris and thrust again until I came hard and long. Two of his fingers slid up my back passage and the excitement intensified as he worked my body into a state of near frenzy.

I couldn't move as his flesh slapped hard against my buttocks and he grunted and bent over me. I heard myself begging him not to stop, begging him to go deeper and harder. He began to shudder and moan with every deep thrust and whisper in my ear.

"I love to fuck you, Eden. I love to make you come all around my big cock. I love you sucking me. Don't think you'll get much sleep tonight. I've years of dreams to make up for and I'm going to fuck you until I run out of come."

This last was choked off as I came hard for him and he joined me in a frenzy of bucking that left us both breathless and exhausted.

He was true to his word. I woke from another hasty doze into the morning light to find myself sprawled on top of him, his cock still wedged inside me. I combed my fingers through his golden chest hair and purred my appreciation. "Gideon was large, but you are truly massive. How can this be when you are twins?"

Gervase grabbed my chin. His gaze was uncomfortably direct.

"You saw Gideon's cock?"

I nodded and his grip grew tighter. "Gideon fucked you?"

"No!" I pulled away from him, grabbing a sheet to cover my nakedness. "Gideon wouldn't let me touch him at all. He said he wished only to help me."

Gervase leaned back against the headboard and folded his arms over his chest. A muscle moved in his cheek. "And what exactly did he teach you?"

My gaze flew to Gideon's whip that lay in full view on the carpet. Before I could speak, Gervase leaned over the side of the bed. He scooped up the whip and laid it on the brocaded cover between us.

"Well?" Gervase asked.

I bit down on my lip as I focused on the whip. "You have to understand, Gervase, that I haven't been properly bedded by a man for three years. Gideon understood about my husband and offered to teach me ways to increase my own pleasure."

"With that?" Gervase pointed at the whip and I started to blush. He began to laugh. "Eden, after all we have done together, you are embarrassed to tell me that Gideon introduced you to the joy of sex toys?"

I blushed even more. Gervase caught my hand, his voice suddenly serious. "I should be thankful for Gideon's aid, if I were you. You would never have been able to take me with such expertise if you hadn't had a man inside you for three years."

Relief rushed through me and I managed to look directly at him. He smiled and drew back the covers to display his massive erection. He brought the whip handle alongside himself and pretended to frown.

"You won't need the whip again, Eden. I think I can fill you much better."

I nodded, dry mouthed as despite its soreness my body responded to his dominant presence. My nipples hardened into tight buds. I gently stroked my fingers over them, enjoying the anticipation. Gervase lay down on his back like a sultan and beckoned me forward. I crawled up his magnificent body until I sat astride him. His cock was so long it nudged between my breasts.

He slid a finger inside me to gauge my readiness and showed me it was soaked.

"You are always wet for me." He put his finger into my mouth and I sucked on it, enjoying the taste of my arousal. I squeezed my breasts together, trapping his cock, and bent my head to lick him with the tip of my tongue.

His breath caught as I came up on my knees and positioned him at the entrance to my passage. He caught my wrist and I stilled when I saw he held the whip. His thumb made lazy circles on my clitoris and his gaze was heavy lidded with desire. He whispered, "How about both? My cock and the whip?"

I gazed down into his eyes as he eased the head of the whip handle against the underside of his cock and clamped his hand around both. "Come on, then," he murmured, "let's see how you do."

Chapter Four

ဢ

I lay back in the rose-scented water and relaxed my sore muscles as I watched Gervase shave. He had just quit the bath and was naked under his thin black silk robe. I enjoyed looking at him. There was not a single piece of fat on his lean hard body unlike Gideon who had begun to soften with his more indolent lifestyle.

There was a discreet tap on the door, and after a quick glance at me, Gervase bade the person enter. I relaxed back against the side of the bath as Gideon sauntered in and winked at me.

"Might I assume you two have made up?"

Gervase grunted as he carefully scraped his cut-throat razor over his chin. I gave Gideon my best smile as he crossed the Persian carpet to sit by the side of the bath.

"I thought we might spend the next few days together in London," Gideon said as he crossed one elegant ankle over the other. "At my expense, of course. Eden needs a new wardrobe now that she is out of mourning and a few days to enjoy society." He inclined his head in my direction. "And as Gervase wants to enjoy you, Eden, I suspect he will be happy to spend his leave with us. Are you both agreeable?"

Gervase grunted again, which both Gideon and I took for assent. My excitement must have shown as Gideon caught my hand and kissed my fingers. Then he reached for the washcloth that hung over the edge of the tub and smiled at me.

"Shall I scrub your back?"

I leaned forward and presented him with the graceful curve of my spine and he began to wash me with languid circular strokes.

After a while, Gideon inquired, "Might I massage your shoulders for you, Eden? You are probably a little stiff after last night's activities."

I pointed to a jar of rose-scented oil that stood by the bath and surrendered myself into Gideon's skillful hands. The scraping sounds of Gervase's shaving ceased and I sneaked a glance across to where he sat. His eyes were fixed on Gideon's fingers as they circled my naked shoulders and skimmed my collarbone.

"Lower."

Gervase's stark command sounded curiously hoarse and Gideon's hands stilled.

"Go lower, Gideon."

I sighed as Gideon added more oil to his fingers and massaged it into my breasts. Gervase swung around in his seat until he faced us. Gervase's cock had risen and fought its way through the confines of his robe. I moved my head slightly to one side and rested my cheek against the front of Gideon's equally straining breeches.

"Get her out of there, Gideon. Put her on the bed."

Gideon slid one hand down into the water and cupped me between the legs. I pressed against his palm, adding even more thick moisture with my instant excitement. He lifted me and laid me gently on the newly made bed. Gideon sat beside me and continued to massage the oil into my heated breasts.

Gervase quit his seat and stood over us, a dark powerful figure at the side of the bed.

"Lower."

He again directed Gideon who obliged by sliding his oil-soaked fingers down over my stomach to rest in my nest of curls. My eyes locked with Gervase's as Gideon pleasured me, his thumb circling my clitoris, his fingers slipping in and out of me as I slowly grew hot and wet and ready to explode.

"Enough," Gervase growled with all the menace of the alpha male.

Gideon withdrew his hand just as I was about to come and, with a shrug in my direction, he relinquished me into Gervase's care. He hadn't reached the door before Gervase moved to cover me. He slid inside with one smooth movement of his hips. I squeezed my internal muscles around his immense presence to hold him deep where I needed him.

"I'll expect you downstairs for dinner then." Gideon's amused voice floated over us but this time Gervase didn't even bother to grunt and I was too busy moaning with pleasure to answer him.

Sometime later, when we had exhausted our passions, I lay curled against Gervase's chest, breathing in his unique scent. Something Gideon had said floated into my mind.

"Do you have to leave soon, Gervase?"

Gervase shifted against the pillows and propped an arm under his head so that he could look down on me. He half-smiled at me, relaxing the strong line of his jaw.

"I have to go back to France, love. Don't you ever read the newspapers? Napoleon has escaped and seeks to re-form his armies and make himself Emperor again." His mouth hardened and for the first time I glimpsed the soldier beneath the sensualist. "I fear there will be a battle to end all battles before the year is out."

I came up onto my knees and stared down at him. "You will fight?"

His eyebrow shot up. "Of course I will." He swept me a makeshift bow. "Major Gervase Harcourt, at your service, ma'am." His gaze roved over my nakedness and he pretended to leer. "Definitely at your service."

His expression sobered as I reached out to touch his smooth cheek. "Some of our crack regiments have been sent overseas to America. We can only hope someone has the sense to call them back before it is too late."

I sat back and looked at him. How could he contemplate exposing his body to musket fire, swords and cannon balls without fear? With an inarticulate cry, I threw myself over him in a vain attempt to offer him my protection.

"I want you to stay here. I don't want you to die."

His deep laugh rumbled through his chest and he stroked my hair. "I appreciate your concern, love, but I expect to survive." He laid me back on the bed and leaned over me, his blue eyes intent. "There is another thing we need to discuss before I give in to my urge to fuck you again." He hesitated for a moment as if searching for the right words. "I have spilled my seed in you. You might bear my child."

Time seemed to stop as I fought to breathe and protect myself from his gaze. I'd forgotten that he didn't know of my deepest shame. I turned away and buried my face in the pillow. His hand fell heavily on my shoulder and twisted me around to face him.

I struggled hard not to give into the temptation to cry. "I do not think I can have children. I was barren during my marriage and my husband never let me forget it."

Gervase's hand gentled on my arm and he stroked my shoulders in reassuring circles. His next question was quiet. "What do you mean?"

"Your father arranged my marriage with Mr. Carstairs because I was young and because Mr. Carstairs desperately wanted a legitimate son. In truth, I have always wanted a family of my own. The thought of a child, even Mr. Carstairs' child, was a welcome one."

I bit down on my lip as I strove to give Gervase the truth. "At first, he was forgiving when I did not conceive. Eventually he began to blame me.

"Then, my husband, began to have difficulties in bed with me." Gervase nodded and I thanked God that I was with the only person in the world who would accept my telling of the story and with whom I didn't need to feel embarrassed.

"He couldn't get hard and naturally he decided it was my fault." I took a deep breath. "One night he slapped me across the face and said I had cursed him." I laughed with no humor in it. "Of course, because he had gotten angry he managed to get hard enough to force himself inside me. Unfortunately that made everything worse."

I sensed that Gervase had gone still. I could no longer look at him as I rushed to complete my sordid tale. I focused on his bare shoulder where a puckered scar spoke of an old sword wound.

"As he became ill and grew older, it became more difficult for him to perform so he hit me harder." I shivered and Gervase gripped my hand. "He broke two of my ribs once and then he started to..." I covered my mouth with my hands.

Gervase rolled me onto my front and ran his fingers along the faded scars that crisscrossed my back.

"I thought you had been beaten, but I wasn't sure who had done it to you. For all I know, it might have been my father." His hand stilled on my back and the warmth from his palm seeped through my shivering skin. "You said that your husband was failing in health, so who beat you?"

My throat dried and I tried to shift away, hoping that he would disappear or that some miracle would stop me from having to answer him. I was rotated onto my back with surprising speed. I still tried to avoid looking at him. He caught my chin in ungentle fingers.

"Eden, who beat you?"

I couldn't look away, even when his hard face blurred and dissolved behind my tears. "His bastard son." I tried to wipe away some of the tears that fell down my face. "I was always afraid that my husband would let his son bed me too, but he was too proud to resort to that, for which I am thankful."

45

My tears ceased and I could see Gervase clearly again. My breath caught in my throat at his deadly expression.

"What is his name?"

"Gervase..." I stroked his arm, his muscles were rigid with tension. "He is dead. It doesn't matter now. I was just trying to explain that I might not be able to have children."

"Not your husband." Gervase said through his teeth. "I want the bastard who dared to lay hands on you. I'll kill him." Gervase pulled me into his arms and held me so close I could scarcely breathe. I struggled until he allowed me to lift my face to his. I kissed his mouth. The tension that radiated through him gradually disappeared. He kissed me back.

Gervase sighed. "You did not deserve this. I wish that I could take back the past miserable years and make them right for you. I feel so damn guilty."

I kissed him again and whispered, "You were not to know your father would discover us together or that Mr. Carstairs would prove to be a difficult husband. But we are here now until you must return to do your duty. Let us enjoy what we have."

He held me away from him for a moment and searched my face. His mouth settled into a determined line. "Only if you promise that if you do carry my child and I am still away that you will tell Gideon and he will aid you."

"I promise." It was a promise easily made and unlikely, to my abiding sorrow, to be called upon.

"Good girl." Gervase drew me beneath him and spread my legs. "Now, I have something to keep you busy until dinner time." He flexed his hips and filled me slowly, watching me the whole time. I drew my knees up to accommodate him and he whispered as he began to move with sensuous ease. "This time I will keep you safe, love, never doubt it."

For the first time in my life I tried to bury my fears and believe that the man who fitted against me with such perfect ease and who understood me better than anyone would keep his promise.

Chapter Five

ℭ

"Are you ready, Eden?"

I drew in a deep breath and placed one gloved hand on each of the twins' arms. The ballroom below me seemed overfull and overloud to my provincial eyes. Only the comfort of knowing I looked my best in a soft mauve silk gown cut in the latest fashion convinced me to keep going. And, of course, the beauty of my two escorts, one in dark blue silk and the other in his best scarlet and gold dress uniform.

Gideon squeezed my hand as our plump hostess came to greet us and to exclaim over my appearance. As Gideon replied with easy grace, Gervase bent to whisper in my ear.

"I'll wager that we'll have all the hopeful bachelors and widowers swarming around us when they hear that you are available again. You know how popular a desperate young widow can be."

With surprising firmness, the twins cleared a path for me through to the edge of the dance floor. A stately country dance was in progress. To my surprise, I even recognized some old acquaintances. Gideon elbowed his way through the crowd to obtain some refreshments and the band struck up a waltz. Gervase bowed low over my hand.

"May I have the pleasure of this dance, Mrs. Carstairs?"

I gave him my best curtsey and slipped gracefully into his arms. My long white gloves showed to advantage against his scarlet sleeve and my body was so well aligned with his that we fell into step with great ease. For a while, I was content just to drift to the music and enjoy the sensation of being held in his arms. I glanced up to find him smiling at me.

"What is it?"

Gervase didn't answer as he negotiated us around a tricky corner and a couple who appeared to be dancing to a different orchestra.

"Gervase?"

He smiled then, showing his white even teeth. I felt a familiar lick of heat pool in my stomach.

"I was remembering learning to waltz together at Harcourt Hall when your hair was still in pigtails."

I smiled back at him as he executed another faultless turn. "I remember it too, I had the bruises to prove it. Gideon had the lighter touch and you trampled my feet unmercifully." I looked down at my unmarked lavender kid slippers. "I am glad to see you have improved."

"You can thank the army for that," Gervase replied. "The Duke of Wellington insists that his staff officers can dance properly."

His remark drew my eye to the number of men in uniform in the ballroom and my feet faltered for an instant. Gervase shifted his hand and rubbed his thumb against the bare skin above my glove as though he sensed my unease.

"I was thinking of something else. How long it will be before I can be inside you again."

I glanced around but nobody seemed to be interested in our low-voiced conversation. I smiled back at Gervase and licked my lips.

"How strange that we think so alike, Major Harcourt. I was just wondering why it feels so peculiar to have clothes on and not to have you buried deep inside me."

Gervase sucked in a breath and under the pretext of a missed step let his lower body grind against mine. He was already aroused and frowned down at me as I continued to smile.

"Don't play games with me, Eden—unless you want to find yourself flat on your back in the next five minutes."

"And how would you manage that in such a public place?" I inquired sweetly. "Do you think we are invisible?"

The music ended and I sank to my knees in a graceful curtsey until my mouth was level with his groin. I blew a hot steam of breath out through pursed lips as I began to rise again. Gervase hissed a curse.

"Is that a challenge?" he murmured as he gripped my arm and towed me off the dance floor in the direction of Gideon who stood conversing with a lady with striking auburn hair. I came to an abrupt halt and bumped my hip against Gervase's groin.

The lady slipped away before I could ask Gideon to introduce her to me, her posture stiff with annoyance. Gervase demanded Gideon's attention.

"Dance with Eden, Gideon, and try to stop her seducing anyone, will you?" He glared at me, a distinct sensual provocation in his eyes. "She seems a little overexcited tonight."

With a curt bow, he stalked off towards a cluster of red coats near the gaming room. I took Gideon's proffered arm and curtsied to him as the musicians played the opening chords of a country dance. It took me a while to forget Gervase's challenge and to notice that Gideon was unusually quiet. His attention seemed fixed on the woman with the glorious auburn hair who danced past us with another scarlet-coated army officer.

"Gideon, who was the lady you were speaking to when Gervase interrupted you?"

"No one of import, at least to you," Gideon replied shortly, without a hint of his usual charm. "If she approaches you, be wary. She seems to think you are my mistress."

"Ah, she is a friend of Georgiana's then?" He nodded as the woman passed us again, her eyes flicking to Gideon's in a distinctly inviting look, which he failed to return.

I sensed that I would get no further with Gideon and wisely chose another topic, which made the dance pass in a far livelier fashion until he escorted me to a chair on the edge of the dance floor.

To my surprise, Gervase proved correct. I was soon surrounded by a bevy of eager would-be suitors and a few old friends who wished to become reacquainted. The evening passed quickly until Gervase appeared at my elbow when supper was announced. In his usual forceful manner he rushed me through the line, collected our plates and two glasses of champagne and hustled me out onto the deserted balcony. With typical arrogance, he shut the glass doors behind him to discourage any other guests from following us out.

I sipped at my champagne and marveled at the freedom I had as a widow compared with an unmarried girl. I could never have been left alone with a man like this before, especially a dangerous, dashing man like Gervase.

I glanced at Gervase as he lit a cigar and leaned over the parapet to view the gardens below. His hair shone guinea gold in the moonlight and his six-foot-two frame showed to advantage in his formal dress. I wandered over to stand beside him. The urge to touch him too strong to resist.

Fairy lights had been strung along the pathways and several couples were taking the air. A light hum of chatter rose to our level like the babbling of a brook. After a quick look around I realized that we were screened from the majority of the house by the angle of the building and that we were completely alone.

I edged in front of Gervase and sank to my knees, my silken skirts billowing around me like a flower. He stared down at me as I released the buttons on his breeches and caressed his rapidly growing cock. I cupped his balls with one hand, took the rest of him into my mouth and sucked deeply.

"Christ, Eden."

His breathing became ragged and his hips began to thrust forward in time with the movements of my mouth. "There are people down in the garden below us."

I didn't bother to reply. I was too busy enjoying the sensation of his cock in my mouth and the many many ways I could use my tongue, teeth and lips to torment him. His fingers crept into my hair and he shuddered like a man possessed as he came down my throat in huge pumping waves.

I reached into his coat pocket and retrieved his handkerchief. I wiped my mouth and rose gracefully to my feet just as I heard the chattering voices of an approaching couple.

"Eden..." Gervase's voice was strained and full of promised revenge. I avoided his outstretched hand as I curtsied and then headed back towards the ballroom in desperate need of something less salty to drink.

Gideon handed me into the carriage with a flourish and Gervase followed me in. Gideon shut the door from the outside, leaving me alone with his brother. Gervase gave me a devilish smile as the carriage moved away from the well-lit mansion.

"So?" Gervase asked, "Did you enjoy yourself?"

I sighed and smiled blissfully back at him. "Yes, it was almost the perfect evening." I glanced up at him under my lashes. "Particularly my supper."

Gervase raised one eyebrow and beckoned me to sit beside him. "You enjoyed tormenting me, then?"

I didn't bother to reply, I just kissed him on the mouth. His fingers slid inside my cloak and unlaced my gown.

"Take this dress off, and your petticoats. We are going to have a little adventure."

Full of anticipation, I complied as Gervase fished a half mask out of his pocket and bade me put it on. For the rest of the journey he arranged me on his lap so that I straddled his cock but despite my urging he refused to undo his breeches. When the carriage stopped we were in a discreet street of fairly new houses towards Hyde Park.

My long cloak covered my lack of clothing. Gervase took my arm and knocked on a discreet door set in the basement of the white stucco house. We were admitted and Gervase paused to remove his cloak, gloves and hat. While he conversed with the footman, I took the opportunity to gaze around the dimly lit passageway.

When Gervase returned to me, I grabbed his arm and hissed, "Is this a whorehouse?"

Gervase had the gall to laugh as he urged me onwards towards a staircase.

"It is a different kind of pleasure house open to wealthy men and women. The woman who opened it, Madame Desiree, wanted to create a place where anyone could come and act out their sexual fantasies in a safe environment."

I dug in my heels. "And what are we doing here?"

Gervase bent and kissed me hard on the mouth. "Doing what you love best, Eden...watching."

We mounted the wide staircase. I gazed at the crimson silk covered walls, which were but an insignificant backdrop for the erotic paintings and sculptures that lined the massive hallway. Thick rugs covered the wooden floors and in two corners of the receiving room, cushions were piled high and people reclined in the manner of a sultan's harem. A selection of couches and chairs filled the rest of the space. Some of them were already occupied.

My steps slowed again as I realized that Gervase seemed very sure of his way. He looked down at me and seemed to anticipate my question.

"Yes, I have been here before, but not for a long while, now come on."

I followed him towards the far end of the saloon where a set of double doors led into a long pink-carpeted corridor. Just before I reached the doors, I heard a moan and looked to the sofa on my left where a well-dressed woman sucked the breast of another woman. I looked closer and blushed to see that the first woman had her hand up the second's skirts.

Gervase stood behind me, his arms wrapped around my waist, and watched as well. His hand crept within my cloak and caressed the tip of my breast.

"Would you like to try that, Eden? I might be persuaded to watch if you wanted to experiment with your own sex."

I tore my gaze away from the entwined pair and moved on, Gervase's hand at my elbow. The light in the corridor was softer and the thick carpet muffled sound. I stopped in front of the first door and read out loud.

"Tales from the Bible."

I looked up at Gervase, full of curiosity. He kissed my hand. "Why don't we go in?"

He opened the door and ushered me inside. It took me a while to focus in the darkness as Gervase handed me into a chair and stood behind me. My gaze riveted on the center of the room where a naked, long-haired woman toyed with an apple. She didn't speak as she rubbed the apple over her body, concentrating on her nipples.

Gervase whispered in my ear, "We have arrived just in time for the beginning of the story. This must be Eve." He bit down on my neck and opened my cloak. One of his hands fastened on my breast and the other slid between my legs.

He squeezed me hard, the gold metal of his signet ring cold against my already moist flesh. "Ah...my own Garden of Eden."

I looked around but the rest of the audience was swathed in blackness so I relaxed into Gervase's touch.

There were muted gasps from the audience as a trap door opened in the floor and a naked man painted red with horns on his head slithered on his belly towards Eve. Gervase grazed my ear with his teeth and then murmured, "I wonder what he'll use for the snake?"

I shushed him as Eve gasped and sat down with her back to the fake glade of trees, her legs falling apart to display her shaven mound. The man stood over her and began to stroke his cock, which had indeed been painted to look like a snake. When fluid started to drip from the tip, he moved closer to Eve and brushed his erection against her closed mouth.

I began to feel warm and shifted slightly in my seat as Eve tilted her head back and allowed the man to push into her mouth. Her hand moved and jammed the apple between her legs in time to the devil man's thrust. Gervase breathed hard in my ear and began to push his fingers inside me to the rhythm being played out on the stage.

The pounding of my heart increased and I realized that the beat of real drums and the cries and groans of the rest of the audience were echoing it. The devil man's buttocks pumped and pumped until he was covered in a fine sheen of sweat. He roared out in triumph over Eve as he came into her mouth and she apparently came too, the apple all but disappearing inside her.

Lights went out over the stage area but there was no applause as the people in the audience concluded or commenced their own performances. Gervase removed his fingers.

"Come on," he said, "there's much more to see." He tugged on my hand and we left, almost tripping over a couple who had decided to fornicate in front of the door. I pulled my cloak around me as we paused in the quiet corridor, my mind reeling from the experience. I glanced at Gervase who was smiling and pulled him against me.

I stood on tiptoe in an effort to get his groin where I wanted it but I was far too short. Gervase grinned and lifted me until my thighs fitted around his hips. I reached down to unbutton his breeches but he stopped me.

"Wait a moment, love. I need to see how wet you are."

I waited with ill-concealed lust as he slid two fingers inside me and closed his eyes. He gave a sigh and shook his head as he lowered me to the ground.

"I'm sorry, but you'll have to get much wetter than that before I'll fuck you."

"Gervase!" I hissed as two masked couples passed us in the hallway and I realized we were in a very exposed place. I lowered my voice. "You know damned well that I am ready for you." I smoothed the front of his tented breeches with my palm. "And you are definitely ready for me. Is this some kind of game?"

"Why, yes. I always forget how astute you are, Eden." He kissed me thoroughly until I struggled to be free. "Consider it a lesson in patience." He watched me through narrowed eyes. "I want you so desperate for me that you'll beg for my cock, that you'll let me fuck you anywhere."

I stared at him and some part of me knew that I should slap his face and walk away. The treacherous wave of lust that curled through me making me wet and wanting told me otherwise. We would see who ended up begging.

"There is something else I think you will enjoy at the Shakespeare room."

I followed Gervase meekly down the corridor until we came to the right door. I sensed that the room and the audience were bigger as we eased our way into the darkness. He secured a chair and sat down on it with me on his lap, turning me until I straddled him and faced the stage.

The stage contained a large four-poster bed hung with silken draperies on which languished another fair-haired woman in a diaphanous nightgown.

"That must be a wig," Gervase whispered. He pointed to her crotch. "See? Her hair is thick and dark there."

A door to the side of the bed opened and a huge dark-skinned man entered wearing little but a loincloth and a ferocious scowl.

"Othello," I breathed as he brandished a handkerchief at the woman who played his Desdemona and she began to shake her head. She slid from the bed and clasped Othello around the knees, dislodging his inadequate loincloth. There was an appreciative feminine gasp from the audience when his enormous shaft was revealed. Somebody moaned.

Desdemona reached for him and rubbed and sucked him until he seemed twice as big. With a growl and another set of screams from the female element of the audience, Othello dragged Desdemona to the bed, bent her over onto her stomach and buried himself deep inside her again and again.

My throat dried as I watched the incredible flex of muscle and strength of the man's back. His muscles gleamed like polished ebony and his buttocks begged to be shaped and touched. A gush of wetness surprised me as my body reacted to his climax.

Gervase's amused voice startled me.

"You like this, don't you?" He brushed his fingers over my soaked pussy and I squirmed with frustrated desire. "Now wait and see what happens next."

Unlike the previous show, the actors didn't leave the stage when the lights were turned up. The Othello character moved to the edge of the stage with easy grace and was soon engulfed by a crowd of women who touched him everywhere. Several men clustered around Desdemona and touched her too.

"Watch," Gervase said again as one of the women, more daring than the others, fell to her knees and took the actor's cock into her mouth. I stared hard at him as his hips moved in time to her mouth and he began to sweat even more. Our eyes locked for a strangely intimate moment as he groaned deep in his throat and came into her mouth. He scarcely glanced at the woman who had pleasured him or at the optimistic woman who was about to take her place.

In the background, I watched as another woman donned the Desdemona costume and laid herself out on the bed, her face flushed and eager. I leaned back towards Gervase.

"Does the Othello character do this all night to an ever-changing parade of Desdemonas?"

Gervase's hand tightened on my breast. "Why? Do you wish to take a turn? It could be arranged."

I wiggled harder on his lap, grinding my hip into his swollen cock and smiled. "No thank you. You are just as big as him and in my experience just as insatiable. Why should I bother?"

Some of the possessive tension disappeared from his face. He smiled back at me. "Why indeed? Except you'll not have me tonight unless you beg."

I slid from his lap, making as much of a meal of it as possible. He swore under his breath.

"There's always Gideon's whip."

I returned to the corridor and Gervase guided me back to the main saloon, which had filled up considerably since our arrival. Several couples lay sprawled against the floor cushions or in the couches, most of them in a state of undress. The scent of sex mingled with women's perfume, smoke from the fire and a buffet laid out in an alcove.

Gervase took my arm and steered me towards the food. "Have you noticed that only some of the women are masked? The rest are courtesans and thrill seekers who don't care who sees them."

I nodded as my fascinated gaze fastened on an acquaintance of my mother's who was being energetically fucked by a man young enough to be her son. The long ostrich feathers in her hair swept down towards the floor and bobbed in time to the man's staccato thrusts.

Eden's Pleasure

So engrossed was I by this spectacle that I did not at first notice the woman who appeared on Gervase's right until he greeted her then turned to me.

"Mrs. C., I would like you to meet Madame Desiree, the clever lady who dreamed up this scheme."

I nodded my head at the woman in front of me, surprised by the warmth of Gervase's tone. Madame Desiree seemed scarce old enough to have managed such an enterprise and far too beautiful to have the brains for it. Although we were similar in height and shape, her coloring was the complete opposite of mine. Where I was dark, she was fair, my eyes were green and hers were blue.

She held out her hand to me and after a slight hesitation I took it. She studied me closely and then glanced up at Gervase.

"I apologize for staring at you but you look somewhat familiar." She laughed lightly at Gervase's guilty expression. "Do not worry, my friend, your secrets are safe with me." She patted his arm. "I am just glad to see you have brought someone special with you tonight."

She squeezed my hand. "Gervase and his brother were the first people I called upon when I needed to finance my house of dreams."

I nodded and withdrew my hand as she turned to pinch Gervase on the cheek. "Well, cheri, are you going to play your favorite part tonight or are you sampling new experiences with your new lady?"

For once, Gervase looked a little unsettled.

"We are alighting where the fancy takes us, Desiree. Have you any suggestions?"

Madame Desiree gave a soft laugh and blew us a kiss. "Alas no, my dears. How would I know your secret fantasies? The choice is yours, always yours."

I watched her drift away amongst her guests as Gervase busied himself at the buffet table. He headed towards a vacant couch and I followed, slapping away an amorous drunk's hand that crept up my leg. I let Gervase settle himself before I asked.

"What part do you always play, Gervase?"

He glared at me over the rim of his champagne glass and swallowed the contents in one gulp. He glanced around the room and returned his gaze to mine with obvious reluctance.

"Would you like to sit in my lap again, Eden? You can beg me to fuck you now."

I laughed, leaned forward and stroked my hand down the front of his breeches. "If you tell me what your favorite role is, I might just do that."

Gervase sighed. "All right." He grabbed my hand and marched me towards the pink carpeted corridor. He stopped outside a door marked "Here be Dragons" and drew me inside. Two characters already stood on the stage. A man dressed in the armor of a medieval knight, his face all bloody, and a woman in a linen shift.

I sank into the nearest seat and stared openmouthed at the woman. Whether she wore a wig or not, she bore a remarkable resemblance to me. Gervase swore softly beside me.

"Damnation, I thought she would have been replaced by now."

I put my hand over his mouth as the woman helped the knight to remove his armor. Then he got into the large wooden bath and she leaned over him, soaking her thin linen shift with the water. She spent a long time washing him and caring for his wounds, stopping frequently to kiss his face and allow him to touch her breasts. Eventually, the knight responded by pulling her into the bath on top of him and making love to her.

I tried to imagine Gervase playing the wounded knight and found it all too easy. He was a soldier, well used to battle and well deserving of comfort. I turned to look at him and found his face unusually still as he watched the woman tend to her knight. Had he come here and thought of me? Had he wanted me to offer him comfort in the past war-torn years?

With aching tenderness, I drew his head down and kissed his warm generous mouth as the woman on the stage gasped and moaned her pleasure.

"Now, Gervase," I whispered. "I'm begging you now."

In answer, he swept me up in his arms and hurried me towards the exit. While we waited for his carriage to be brought around, he held me pressed against the wall, my face buried against his muscular chest. I could feel his heartbeat and the pulse of his arousal through the thin black silk of my undergarments.

The carriage arrived and he handed me inside with a terse command to his coachman.

"Drive around until I tell you to stop."

Without further words, he opened his breeches and his cock sprang free. He dragged me astride him and, with a hoarse sound of need, entered me with one swift upward thrust. I wrapped my arms and legs around him as I sought to adjust to his hard length. The carriage picked up speed and rocked me closer into his arms.

I purred with pleasure as he pumped into me, dug my heels into the seat and arched my spine. He kept up the demanding pace and depth of his thrusts until I came hard and wet around him. He gave me no respite but rode me through the pleasure until it began to peak again. His mouth latched onto my silken-clad breast and suckled me without ceasing.

I screamed then and he growled. "Yes, scream again, I want my coachman to hear you and get hard wishing he could have you."

I tried not to but Gervase was a demanding lover. My body lapped up the pleasure he gave me until I didn't care if the Prince Regent himself heard my moans of delight.

"Again."

He urged me on despite me begging him not to, one set of fingers twisting my nipple, the other rubbing my clitoris as he pounded into me. I came again, and with a groan he followed me into the realm of pleasure we had created together.

As I slumped, exhausted against his chest, he thumped on the carriage roof with his cane and we soon arrived at Gideon's house. Gervase gave me no opportunity to aid myself, he simply picked me up in his arms, carried me into the house and deposited me in my bed.

I watched with a ripple of anticipation as he stripped off his clothes and came down over me. He removed the wisps of lace and silk, which were all that remained of my underthings after his rough handling, and stared down at me. Leaning across, he brought a branch of lit candles closer to the bed.

"Open your legs, Eden."

I whimpered as his finger sought entrance to my swollen passage. He smiled softly, his face illuminated in the candlelight.

"You think you are too sore to take me again?"

I nodded as his fingertips dabbled in the thick and seemingly endless stream of his seed that ran down between my legs. "How long do you think it will take me to get inside you again?"

I shuddered at the feather light touch of his fingertips caressing me so carefully but didn't answer.

Gervase continued to touch and to talk.

"Do you remember when we met in the barn at Harcourt Hall farm? You had grown up considerably since we had last seen you. Who did you prefer to watch, Gideon or me?"

"You..." I gasped as he swirled his thumb over my clitoris, barely touching it.

"Why?" he asked idly. "What was it that I did that Gideon didn't?" Gervase slid downwards and commanded. "Touch your breast for me, Eden, while I attend to your pussy."

I tried to think back as Gervase licked his way up my thigh. The tip of his tongue flicked lightly against my engorged clitoris with masterly restraint. I stroked my nipple in time with Gervase's licks and started to feel warm again. "Gideon never seemed to enjoy himself as much as you did. He seemed to make all the right gestures and then seemed disappointed or bored by the final act."

I squirmed as Gervase drove his tongue deeper and I felt myself opening up to him like a flower. He brought his dripping face up for a second and shook his head like a dog. His teeth gleamed white in the candlelight.

"How very perceptive of you, Eden." He glanced at the clock on the mantel. "Five minutes to make you soaking wet and fuckable, love. You are far too easy."

I tried to struggle out of his grasp as he knelt up to show me his straining cock. He laced my fingers with his and wrapped them around the huge base as he positioned himself between my legs.

"Don't look so annoyed. I wasn't trying to be insulting. After all, you do the same to me." He glanced down at his cock and grimaced as he parted my labia and slid inward. "If you think that this is normal for a man after the night we've had, you will be sorely disappointed. I've never been this insatiable before, and like you, I will pay for it in the morning."

The thick base of his shaft nudged my pussy. He groaned and ground his hips hard against mine. He chuckled into my neck. "Just be thankful that unlike me, you do not have to go on duty and sit astride a horse for four hours tomorrow morning. Promise me that you will not walk past headquarters tomorrow. God help me if I think of you then!"

Chapter Six

🙰

I sat at my dressing table and reread the note delivered to the house that morning. I was not surprised that the viscount had discerned my whereabouts. He always seemed to know my secrets. Rumor had it that his association with the Foreign Office during the war had resulted in a number of captured French spies and thwarted plots. Keeping an eye on one wayward female relation probably seemed easy by comparison. With a deep breath, I looked at my suddenly pale face in the mirror. The twins' father was back in London and wished me to present myself at his dwelling on the morrow.

My idyllic days with Gervase were drawing to a close. I was not sure whether to be glad or sorry. He had stirred unwelcome emotions in me that I had sworn to forgo. My hands clenched on the note and my green eyes darkened and reflected my anguish. I could not bear to be in love with Gervase again. I could not allow myself to be left desolated by his desertion.

I smoothed powder onto my face and rose to my feet, suddenly needing to be outside. A walk through the tranquil glades of Hyde Park seemed necessary to soothe my agitation and to give me time to formulate my plans for the future.

I strolled through the park. My maid followed at a discreet distance. I scarcely saw the beauty of the emerging leaves and the bitter, sweet, sharp colors of spring. Could I face another elderly husband after Gervase? Other desperate or clever women had chosen this route before me and seemingly felt no compunction in cuckolding their elderly partners with a succession of eager young lovers.

I shook my head. My experiences with Mr. Carstairs had made me wary of such an arrangement.

I looked up as a pigeon disturbed the leaves on a cherry tree. A fistful of pink blossoms floated to the ground around me like a shower of bridal confetti. What if Gervase asked me to be his mistress and suggested he set me up in my own establishment? I came to a halt as a wave of misery washed over me. No, I could not accept that either, despite my desire for him. It would only prolong the inevitable heartache when he chose to marry some fresh-faced chit straight out of the schoolroom and discarded me.

I resumed my walk. The break would have to be complete for me to bear it. Tears threatened in the corners of my eyes as I contemplated the muddle I had created for myself with such blithe overconfidence. How in God's name could I have thought that going to bed with Gervase again would be anything but heart-wrenchingly wonderful? How could I have believed that I would escape unscathed?

"Excuse me."

I hastily wiped my eyes as I realized I had inadvertently blocked the path. I looked up to apologize and caught my breath as I recognized the hauntingly beautiful auburn-haired woman whom Gideon had warned me against.

She lifted one arched eyebrow and held out her gloved hand. A bronze-colored silk bonnet charmingly framed her pale face.

"I believe you are an acquaintance of Lord Gideon Harcourt. Is that so?"

I touched her fingers with my own as I made a brief curtsey and nodded. "Yes, we are old friends. My mother is his mother's second cousin."

She surprised me by slipping her hand into the crook of my arm and strolling beside me. "Well that is good. When I saw that you had been crying, I wondered if Gideon had been trifling with your affections." She shrilled a laugh, which was sharp enough to set my teeth on edge. "Gideon certainly doesn't visit my bed anymore but I am relieved to hear that he hasn't been breaking your heart in yours."

Despite the apparent ease of her tone, her fingers tightened on my arm. I was glad to exonerate Gideon.

"I am happy to reassure you that Gideon has always been the perfect gentlemen."

Her nails clamped into my skin and her voice came out in a hiss. "Oh yes, Gideon's always so perfect. Too perfect to allow anyone else to make a mistake."

I tried to ease out of her grip, alarmed by the feral glare in her yellowish eyes. She refused to release me. I looked around for my maid, caught her eye and beckoned her closer. I sighed in relief as my maid's presence seemed to release the tension in the woman before me. I made a point of stepping away and smoothing out my sleeve before I turned to confront her.

"Miss…" I stopped in confusion as I realized I didn't know this worrying creature's name. My breath nearly ceased as a flicker of triumph lit her eyes.

"You don't know who I am, do you?"

"All I know is that Gideon told me to keep away from you and now I understand why. You are clearly unstable." I gave her a sharp nod. "Good day to you, whoever you are. I shall definitely heed Gideon's advice from now on."

Her smile grew even wider, exposing her sharp pointed teeth. She began to laugh hysterically.

"Oh, God, this is wonderful. You really don't know who I am, do you?"

I refused to drop my gaze and she gave me a formal curtsey. "I am Lady Harcourt, Gideon's wife."

I pushed past her, my mind in turmoil. Her mocking laughter pursued me through the glade of trees and beyond the cast iron gates of the park.

I joined Gideon and Gervase in the dining room at the appointed hour, dressed in one of my old black gowns. I curtsied to Gideon, accepted an enthusiastic kiss on the cheek from Gervase and allowed them to seat me between them at the table.

Silence fell as the men attacked their food with their usual gusto. I tried to subdue the appalling suspicions my encounter with Gideon's wife had raised in my heart. After a while, when we were settled with our dessert and port, Gideon waved away the servants and we were alone.

I wiped my mouth with my napkin and received a glass of port from Gideon. I caught a searching look of inquiry from Gideon to Gervase and the helpless shrug of Gervase's broad shoulders in response.

"She seems unhappy with us," Gideon remarked.

Gervase half smiled. "I have not quarreled with her, if that's what you are implying." He gave me a sly wink. "She seemed quite well satisfied when I left her in bed this morning."

I half rose to my feet and glared at the pair of them.

"If you insist on speaking about me as if I were invisible, then maybe I will oblige you by retiring."

Gervase stood up, his intention to bar my way clear in his intense blue eyes.

"Eden, if you have something you wish to say, please say it." He spread his hands wide to include Gideon. "We are all friends here, we have no secrets."

"No secrets?" I managed a tight smile and focused my attention on Gideon who sat at his ease at the head of the dining table with his habitual air of distance.

"I too thought that we were friends but I find that I am mistaken. I met your wife in the park today, Gideon." I sought some reaction in Gideon's expression but nothing changed. "Do you remember her? The redheaded woman you warned me to stay away from?"

Gervase opened his mouth and made a sudden movement towards me. I stayed him with a gesture. "Your wife implied that you never bed her and it occurred to me that you never allowed me to touch you either." A muscle twitched in Gideon's cheek as I advanced towards him suddenly furious. "What is it, Gideon? Do you get pleasure from making women beg?" I shot a glance at Gervase. "Or in my case were you merely acting as a procurer for your twin?"

After a hasty shared glance, both men stared at me without speaking. I clenched my fists to contain the pain that threatened to rip through my heart. "Was that all it was? A game to seduce the poor, desperate, pathetically grateful widow? Do you laugh about me behind my back? Do you intend to tell all your friends about me?"

I raised my chin and stared hard at Gideon. "No wonder your wife seems not to care for you. Have you shared her with Gervase too?"

The stem of Gideon's glass snapped between his fingers. Crimson port flooded the white tablecloth like new blood.

"That's enough, Eden." Gideon flung the shattered glass at the wall. His voice was as cold as stone, his expression even harder. He half turned to Gervase. "Get her cloak, Gervase."

Gervase obliged and soon I was traveling in the carriage between the two grim-faced brothers, none the wiser as to my destination.

I was somewhat relieved when the carriage pulled up at Madame Desiree's House of Pleasure. Gideon caught my arm in an iron grip and forced me to keep up with him as we dispensed with the pleasantries and hurried through to the main door-lined corridor. The door Gideon opened and thrust me through bore the legend "Crime and Punishment."

Before I could ask, Gideon pushed me up against a window, which looked down into an opulent bed chamber. He stood behind me, his hands planted on either side of my head so that I could not escape.

"This is one of the more private rooms. We can see in but they cannot see out."

The room seemed modern and unlike the others where Gervase had taken me. My unease deepened when a footman strolled in and began to light the candles. A woman followed him in through the door, her glorious auburn hair loose, her voluptuous figure plainly visible through her silk nightgown.

Gideon stiffened behind me, but I had already identified the woman who claimed to be his wife. I could scarcely bear to watch as she approached the footman and cupped his groin in an unmistakable fashion. To my surprise, the footman resisted her attentions and when she persisted, he slapped her across the face. A red mark appeared on her cheek. I realized with a cold sick feeling that he had truly meant to hurt her and that this was not make believe.

She fell to her knees and opened the footman's breeches. He made no effort to help her until she had exposed his erection and then he dug his fingers into her hair and held her steady while he plunged deep into her mouth. He came fast, forcing her head back with the depth of his thrusts until she seemed certain to choke.

I tried to turn away as she pleaded with him to touch her, clinging to his thigh until he kicked her away from him. Gideon refused to release me despite my struggles and Gervase remained out of my sight.

"This is how Caroline is, Eden," Gideon said roughly. "This is what my wife wants from a man. I refuse to hurt her and thus she brings her sadistic passions here."

I cringed back, although I knew that they could not see me, as another man entered the room. From his rough attire, I guessed he was a stable hand. The footman pointed at the woman who lay at his feet and the stable hand came and stood over her. I stared in disbelief as he too allowed her to suck his cock as the footman watched.

Afterwards, the footman spoke again, seemingly telling Caroline to remove her clothing. She complied with alacrity. I could not believe she enjoyed being shamed and abused by the two servants but her hardened nipples, flushed skin and languorous expression declared otherwise. She stood with her eyes closed as the two men circled her like two ravenous dogs, pinching her breasts, slapping her buttocks and pushing their fingers up inside her.

Her eager expression made me feel sick. I was immeasurably glad when Gideon released me.

"Christ," he muttered as he spun away and punched the door with his fist. "She has got worse."

I turned away from the window and buried my face in Gervase's jacket as the men behind me dragged Gideon's wife towards the bed.

Gideon leaned back against the door, his head tipped back, his hands hidden in his pockets. "When I first married Caroline, I thought she just liked to be bedded a little roughly and I was happy to oblige. But I soon realized she craved more pain and humiliation than I was prepared to give her. When I refused to aid her, she started on the household servants until it became well nigh impossible to keep male staff."

Gideon sighed. "I threatened to cut off her income if she persisted in bringing her perversions home and so she turned to this place. At least I know she is safe here."

"Why don't you divorce her?" I whispered to his averted gaze. "I know that it is difficult to achieve, but with your connections and money, surely you could manage it?"

Gervase drew the crimson curtains across the window as Gideon finally turned to face me.

"Do you think I have not considered it? It is not that simple. She is in a position to blackmail me if I divorce her and she is not very stable. I know she would not hesitate to expose me if she was driven to it."

Gervase put a hand on my shoulder as I stared dry mouthed at Gideon. He crossed his arms across his chest and smiled at me.

"Haven't you guessed? Gervase thought you had. It's quite simple really, I prefer men." He shrugged. "I can perform with a woman if I must. They can even arouse me," he bowed in my direction, "as you well know, Eden. For a while I tried to deny my true feelings and fucked every woman in sight. I also thought it my duty to marry and produce an heir." He frowned down at his boots. "That proved impossible when I realized Caroline was incapable of fidelity and that any child of hers would probably not be mine."

I could only nod as the thousand small unsatisfactory sensual memories we had shared fell into place.

"How did your wife find out?"

"I was indiscreet at a house party and she caught me and my lover." He grimaced in self disgust. "Not before she had provided herself with two witnesses and extracted their written statements, of course."

I moved forward impulsively and hugged him. "Oh, Gideon, you poor thing. What a horrible mess."

I caught a flash of relief in his eyes as he set me away from him. Had he thought I would be disgusted by him?"

As I stared at the twins, an idea came to me which I hoped would wipe out the horrible images we had been forced to endure. I touched Gervase's arm.

"Do you think that Madame Desiree could find us a private room?"

Gervase caught my eye and nodded. "Of course, love. Gideon and I are her favorite customers." He raised an eyebrow at me. "What is it that you plan to do?"

I linked my arm through his and collected Gideon as we left from the room. "You told me that this is the place to act out my fantasies. I have one particular idea that involves you both. Will you help me fulfill it?"

The room Madame Desiree graciously lent us contained all the comforts of a lady's boudoir and a bed big enough for an orgy. Gideon and Gervase stood by the fireplace and I walked across to hand them both a brandy. While they sipped their drinks I started to talk.

"I remember watching you both in the barn one afternoon when you did something I had never seen before." I walked over to Gervase and unbuttoned his jacket, then did the same for Gideon. "You had one of the dairy maids with you, a favorite of yours, called Daisy. Do you remember her?"

A small smile curled Gervase's lip. His eyes met mine in total understanding and apparent approbation of my plan.

"I recall her," Gideon commented softly as I eased him and then Gervase out of their shirts. I paused to circle Gideon's nipples with my fingertip until they hardened. I did the same to Gervase.

I turned my back to allow Gervase to unhook and unlace my dress and petticoats. I slipped my feet out of my shoes and began to work off Gideon and Gervase's boots. I admired the golden hair on the twins' chests and the sight of their cocks straining against their breeches. I made them stand close together so I could rub my palms over their flat furred bellies and firm muscled buttocks.

I took Gervase's hand and placed it on the lacing of my corset and rested Gideon's hand in the small of my back. With a murmur of appreciation, Gervase removed my corset and my breasts swung free. Before he could touch them, I headed for the bed and bade them sit with me.

I crossed my legs and sat up, one knee touching each of the brothers. Gervase's breeches had almost given way under the strain of his massive erection. Taking pity on him and Gideon, I allowed them to remove their breeches. I took off my stockings too, leaving only a thin band of black velvet sewn with pearls around my throat.

I stared hungrily at Gervase's huge cock and my body quivered with the thought that I would soon have him inside me. With a shiver of delight, I licked the tip of my middle finger and pretended to pout. "Let me see if I can remember exactly what I saw. Gideon, you need to sit up against the headboard." He moved up the bed and spread his legs as I came towards him. "And Gervase? You need to be behind me."

Gervase wrapped an arm around my hips with a satisfied grunt. I could already feel his cock jabbing at my wet pussy, demanding entrance. I crawled closer to Gideon and licked my way around his taut balls, nuzzling his crisp golden hair, grazing my teeth against the soft flesh of his inner thigh. He shuddered as I took his cock in my mouth. It grew and thickened against my swirling tongue. Using the tip, I caressed the sensitive slit at the tip of his erection. I took more of him and began to suck with a regular sliding rhythm.

Gervase watched me pleasure his twin, his fingers playing with my swollen bud until with a groan of savage need he thrust blindly inside me. His massive shaft thrust me forward, pressing Gideon deeper into my mouth as he followed my movements.

Gideon dug his fingers into my hair as I increased the pace. I grasped the base of his shaft, holding him still as I felt the first spurt of his seed. My needs narrowed to my desire to make Gideon and Gervase come together until all I could hear were the sounds of flesh slapping or sucking against flesh and the moans of three aroused people.

Gideon came hard and fast into my mouth just as Gervase released himself with a growl. My own climax followed with shocking intensity as I was buffeted between the two men's grinding hips.

For a long while there was silence as we strove to get our breath back. Then Gervase pulled out of me and I felt his seed gush down my thighs. His warm, strong fingers massaged the wetness into my skin. I closed my eyes when another set of hands covered in perfumed oil began to knead my breasts. Blindly, I reached for the bottle and began to massage my two men as well.

Soon we slid and slithered over each other's bodies like a family of playful sea otters. I drowned in the luxury of having two men to pleasure and two huge cocks to play with. Our play became more purposeful as slick fingers pushed inside my pussy, wet tongues licked my clitoris and I grasped and fondled taut buttocks, soft ball sacs and hard, hard shafts.

Gervase lay sprawled on his back. I crawled up him and lowered myself down on his cock. He kissed me hard, his tongue thrusting into my mouth as Gideon lay on top of me, his oiled fingers widening and stretching my back passage. I felt his cock slide a little way inside me. I must have stiffened. Gervase reassured me with his mouth and the subtle undulation of his hips. I relaxed against him. Gideon slid deeper.

"All right?" Gideon whispered as I grew used to the extraordinary sensation of arousal and fullness the twins had given me. I'd never felt so stretched and yet so fulfilled. Could the men feel each other through the fragile skin separating them? The indecent thought inflamed my heated senses and made me crave the erotic experience more.

I nodded and Gideon groaned and slowly thrust downward, his hands anchored on my hips as Gervase thrust upwards. I could do nothing but let the extremity of the sensation roll through me in ever increasing spirals of ecstasy. I started to scream long before they finished with me, my cries muffled on Gervase's oil-soaked chest as I shook with a never-ending climax.

We lay locked together for a long time. I even slept for a while, exhausted by my passions. I awoke to hear Gervase whispering fiercely to Gideon, "I'll not let you have her like this again, Gideon. She's mine from now on, do you understand?"

Gideon kissed my shoulder and slid off me, his reply equally quiet. "I know that, you fool."

I heard him slip on his clothes and leave. I whimpered and cuddled closer to Gervase at the sudden cold.

"Eden, we need to go. Wake up, love."

I opened one eye and regarded him. "Why can't we stay here?" I grumbled and Gervase laughed.

"Because I want to fuck you again and I don't intend to do it until you are in your own bed." I rocked my hips against him and he hissed a curse. His cock started to twitch and grow inside me.

"Why not here?" I kissed the corner of his mouth and he held me away from him. His shaft slid out of me with a soft sucking sound and I pouted.

"Because we need to bathe and get rid of Gideon's scent before I fuck you. You may think me over possessive but I need to make you mine again."

I reluctantly crawled to the edge of the bed and looked for my dress. "Then why did you allow Gideon into our bed?"

Gervase swung his legs over the side of the bed and picked up his shirt, his expression unreadable. "Because he needed you." He paused to pull his crumpled shirt over his head. "Because he is my twin." He stepped into his breeches and fought to close them. "And because I wanted to make sure you really preferred me."

I paused in my dressing, went over to him and put my arms around his neck. "And?" I inquired as he encircled my waist. "Are you satisfied?"

He nodded, his eyes intent on the knot of his cravat. I kissed him full on the mouth. "Thank you for allowing me to fulfill my fantasy. But it's always been you, Gervase, only you."

He grunted, picked up his coat and offered me his arm with a flourish. "All right then, we can stay here but first we must bathe and change."

I bathed alone and readied myself for my last night with Gervase. Tomorrow I had to meet with his father and find out my future but this night belonged to me. It was past midnight when Gervase returned, clad only in a black silk dressing gown, his golden hair damp from the bath.

I walked towards him, the transparent butter soft silk of my borrowed night robe hissing against my skin. He took me into his arms and turned me to face the mirror, his expression serious. I stared at his reflection, noticing how small I looked locked within his muscular arms and how safe I felt.

He whispered against my neck. "Bend forward over the chaise lounge. I must have you quickly."

I leaned forward and his cock nudged my labia and pressed into me. He grabbed my hips and pulled me backwards as he pumped forwards, making each long thrust as deep and as powerful as he could. I held onto the back of the couch and watched him in the mirror. The concentration and primitive lust on his face and the play of his muscles was so erotic that my sheath clenched again and again around him.

He slid two fingers into my back passage and then withdrew his cock from my pussy. I moaned at the loss but he shook his head and plunged his cock in with his fingers, his voice rough in my ear. "Here too, where Gideon was. No other man will come in you again, just me."

He groaned with each stoke and soon came, flooding me with an unending stream of his seed. My legs were trembling when he finally released me and led me over to the bed. He stretched out and lay down on his back and beckoned to me like a king.

Smiling, I knelt over him and he grinned.

"I sense that you are plotting something, Eden. You have an incredibly sensuous gleam in your bewitching green eyes." He raised an eyebrow. "What would you like to do with me? Now that I have gotten over my possessive caveman lust, I am all yours."

I took a deep breath. "Will you let me make love to you, Gervase?"

He regarded me for a long time, his eyes heavy with desire and something else and then nodded. "Of course." He drew his hands over his head and gripped the headboard. "If you truly wish to make this memorable, how about you tie my hands up here? Then I really will be unable to touch you."

The thought appealed to me as Gervase had known it would. I climbed off the bed to find something to bind him with. In a drawer, I found several wide black ribbons. I returned to the bed and used two of the shorter ribbons to tie his wrists to the headboard.

The third I kept in my hand as I knelt up to survey my captive. I leaned over and kissed him gently on the mouth, enjoying the roughness of his unshaven chin and the softness of his lips against mine. I began to work my way down his body, stopping to kiss and nuzzle and worry over every scar that marred his perfection. He spread his legs as I moved over his hard, flat belly, dipping my tongue into his navel, making him squirm.

I avoided his erection and continued to slide my way down to his feet. After kissing and licking the arches of his feet until he pleaded for mercy, I crawled back up and sat between his legs. With a wicked smile, I unfurled the black silk ribbon and held it taut between my two hands. My nipples hardened and showed through the silk as I rubbed it over my breasts. Gervase licked his lips, his attention riveted on the movements of the ribbon.

Then I took the ribbon and wound it lightly around his shaft, covering his flesh. His hips moved restlessly forward as I knelt up, took the end of the ribbon between my teeth and pulled it off in one slow spiraling motion. I did it again and again until the ribbon was stained with his semen and he strained against his bonds.

Leaving the ribbon wrapped tightly around his cock, I ignored his threats and sat facing him, my knees open and overlapping his thighs. Capturing his heated gaze, I stroked my clitoris with one hand and pinched my nipple between my finger and thumb. I rocked back and forth, enjoying the sensation of his coarsely haired thighs against my soft thighs and buttocks.

My excitement grew as lust mounted in his gaze and he was forced to watch me pleasure myself to a climax. His fingers flexed within his bonds. I knew he was trying to break free.

"Eden..." The words sounded as if they had been torn from his throat. "Fuck me, please."

I shook my head and he growled an obscenity. This was my last night with him. I was determined to extract every sensual memory I could from it. Gervase didn't know it yet, but the sight of a beautiful, well-made man with a huge cock tied to my bed begging me to fuck him would have to last me a lifetime.

I unfurled the black ribbon with a flick of my wrist and tied it around my narrow waist. As Gervase watched, I brought the loose end from the back between my legs and secured it at my waist. I crawled up Gervase's body and knelt over his face so that he could see how the ribbon ran between my labia and covered my clitoris and my passage.

I slowly lowered myself down towards his mouth. With a groan he started licking the black ribbon. His tongue probed and curled along the edges, trying to get underneath it, but I pulled it tight.

In desperation, he rubbed his tongue and his unshaven chin against my clitoris until it swelled against the ribbon. Then he sucked both into his mouth, holding on with his teeth. As he pleasured me, I arched backwards, put my hands behind my back and grasped his cock. The second I touched him, he came, soaking my hand. He cursed long and loudly.

I raised myself away from his face before he could attempt any punishment and smiled down at his maddened

Eden's Pleasure

features. His jaw tightened and he whispered, "You little tease. Just you wait until I get my hands free. I'm going to fuck you until you beg for mercy."

I bent and licked his mouth and then bit down hard on his lower lip. "I plan on leaving you tied up all night, so think again."

I slithered down to where his seed lay in pools on his stomach and anointed my breasts with a generous handful until they gleamed and dripped. Then I trailed my nipples over his lips until he took them into his mouth and suckled me.

"See how you taste," I murmured as his cock rose against my naked back, nudging the black ribbon. "I want it all from you, tonight, Gervase. I want to suck you dry."

I braced myself on my knees over him. An expression of relief crossed his face. I lowered myself until the swollen, weeping tip of his arousal brushed against the black silk ribbon. He could go no farther. I moved my hips back and forth, enjoying the sensation and his obvious frustration. I angled my body and slid up and down the sides of his massive erection until he writhed in lack of fulfillment.

My body throbbed with the need to take him but I fought to control myself. I stared at Gervase who was covered in a thin sheen of sweat and even more desirable as a result. I put one finger between my legs and held the ribbon to one side. Gervase stilled as I slowly lowered myself down onto his cock. I came instantly and had to force myself to pull up and away from him.

The expression on his face as I climbed off the bed was indescribable. He roared. "Come back here and finish what you started. Come and fuck me!"

I poured myself a large brandy and sauntered back towards him. "Would you like some of this?"

He shook his head. "No, damn it! I want to fuck you."

79

I sat down next to him and sipped my brandy. Gervase's lust filled eyes narrowed and he fisted his hands.

"What exactly do you mean, Gervase? You have already fucked me several times." I kissed him and allowed some of the brandy to trickle into his mouth. He smiled back at me, showing his teeth. I shifted away. His whole demeanor radiated a primitive rage.

"If I tell you, sweetheart, it won't be a surprise, will it?"

I finished my brandy and paused to unwrap the ribbon from between my legs, desperate to release the throbbing pressure. I quickly straddled Gervase and lowered myself down on him with a grateful sigh. Before I could raise myself up again, Gervase planted his feet firmly on the mattress and pushed upward until his whole lower body came off the bed. With a gasp, I struggled to right myself as he thrust higher and my legs slipped against his hips. It was as exhilarating as trying to master a wild horse. I struggled to stay on top of him as he fought to buck me off.

I knew I was doomed when I heard a harsh ripping sound and Gervase freed his right wrist. With a triumphant roar, he pulled out of me and pressed me face down into the sheets as he busied himself freeing the left.

"Now, my lady," he said breathlessly, "I have the upper hand." He rolled me onto my back and carefully removed the long black ribbon from around my waist. He ripped the ribbon in half with his teeth and dangled the pieces in front of my nose. There was nothing I could do to stop him looping the ribbon around both my wrists and securing it on the headboard. He slid off the bed and went to pour himself a drink before returning to sit beside me.

"Open your legs, Eden."

I did as he commanded, well past modesty now and eager to see what he would do with me. I sighed as his long fingers tugged at the soaking curls in between my legs.

"You are so wet that one might think that you had serviced an entire regiment tonight rather than just one man." I shivered as he circled my swollen bud with the tip of his thumb. "I never imagined I would meet a woman, let alone a lady, who would be able to keep up with my sexual demands, but you not only keep up you exceed my expectations."

He opened my legs even wider and settled between them.

"I think I will dry you off. And then we can start again."

He took the corner of the sheet and wiped away the wetness. He even pushed the fabric inside me to make sure I was completely dried to his satisfaction. When he had finished, he bent forward and kissed me, his rich male scent filled my nostrils. The gentle brush of his cock against my belly made me melt inside.

After a long deep kiss, he sat back, glanced down between my legs and frowned.

"Eden, you are wet again. I'll have to dry you."

I began to sense the game he intended to play as he wiped me dry. He suckled my breasts until the inevitable happened and I grew wet and swollen with need again.

The rasping of the cloth became a torment and a punishment as I strove to remain unaffected by his caresses and kisses but couldn't. I knew I would be wet again as he nudged my mouth with the wet tip of his cock but refused to go inside even when I opened my lips.

As his hand returned between my legs, he pretended to sigh as he drew forth more of my juices and sucked his fingers. I bit down hard on my lip and tried not to stare longingly at his cock as he regarded me.

"What am I to do with you, Eden?"

I refused to answer and he reached for the sheet again. My body squirmed away from him but he captured one of my legs under his heavy thigh. I closed my eyes and listened to the cloth brush against my skin until I thought I might scream.

"If you tell me what you want, love, I might aid you." My eyes flew open as Gervase ran a hand up and down his cock. "After all…" He smiled at me. "It seems a shame to waste this, doesn't it?"

"Yes." I managed to choke out the words. "Yes, damn you. I want you to make love to me."

Gervase's expression changed and he reached up to release my hands. "That's the second time you have said that tonight, Eden. Is fucking not to your liking anymore?"

As the silence lengthened, I silently berated my lack of control. I had promised myself not to mention the word love and had apparently done so twice. Gervase was no fool. I could not judge from his face whether the thought of lovemaking as opposed to fucking meant anything at all to him.

I managed to smile at him and hold out my arms. He came over me and slid into me. I held tightly to his shoulders as relief and pleasure rushed through me in unending pulsating waves. He might call it what he wished but I knew in my heart that I was making love.

Chapter Seven

ဆ

I awoke before dawn and slid from the bed. Gervase lay sprawled on his back, an expression of deep innocence and contentment on his face. I bent to brush a kiss on his roughened cheek and tied one of the black ribbons in a jaunty bow around his softened cock. I stopped at the door to look back at him, knowing that this last sight would have to last me a lifetime. Tears crowded the back of my throat as I pictured the long lonely years ahead.

I blew him a kiss and then hurried home to dress for my visit with the viscount. His note had stated that I visit at my convenience but I knew he meant at my earliest convenience. While I waited for the appropriate social hour to call, I busied myself packing my bags and sending them to a posting house.

I was glad that neither Gideon nor Gervase were at home to see me leave. I doubted if I could have answered their questions with any equanimity. They knew me too well to believe any lies that I might have attempted. I cast one last glance around the sumptuous black marble of Gideon's hallway then squared my shoulders and left for Harcourt House where the twins' father was now in residence.

Viscount Harcourt saw me immediately and I was ushered into the red gold splendor of his study by a butler of truly awe-inspiring dignity. The viscount rose to his feet and bowed to me as he gestured to a straight-backed chair in front of his imposing mahogany desk. I arranged myself on the seat as gracefully as I could, clasping my reticule to disguise my shaking fingers.

The twins' father regarded me over the top of a pair of gold-rimmed spectacles, which did nothing to dispel his air of authority or hide his handsome features. He was dressed in the latest fashion, not a crease visible in the perfect fit of his dove-gray jacket or a fold out of place in his starched cravat.

"Ah, Eden. Thank you for coming to see me."

He smiled and his likeness to his sons became even more apparent. Where their hair was golden, his had faded to a dull straw color, their eyes were bright blue, his were a more cynical silver.

He set down his quill pen and steepled his fingers together. "I hear you have been enjoying your widowhood, my dear, particularly with my sons." He shrugged as if amused. "It is a shame that Mr. Carstairs died so easily and failed you so badly in that area of your marriage."

I stiffened in my chair as I registered the mocking tone of his voice. For a man who had been known as a rake in his youth, and worse, the viscount seemed to have changed his views.

I stared at the pile of books on his desk before I ventured a reply. I did not want to antagonize the viscount when he held my future in his hands but I refused to allow him to intimidate me. I lifted my chin, a false smile pinned to my lips.

"I appreciate your concern, my lord, but Mr. Carstairs was not a kind man and he perhaps came by his just reward."

His silver eyes met mine and reflected my hint of a challenge. "Well, be that as it may, as a favor to your mother, I believe it behooves me to find you another husband." His long fingers stirred some papers on the desk and he glanced down at them. "Unfortunately, Mr. Carstairs did not leave you well enough provided for to allow you to live alone. Of course, if you had had his child, the situation would be different."

I bit down on my lip at this pointed reminder of my failure as the viscount continued speaking. "However, I do have some candidates in mind for you. One of whom my sons insisted I consider."

I gazed at him in bewilderment and his lip curled in apparent surprise. "You did not know? I have had to listen to Gideon and Gervase pleading your case for the last month. Gideon appears to think I should allow you to marry Gervase, presumably because they still feel guilty about what happened to you when you were eighteen."

I found my voice and looked straight back at him. "Perhaps it is right that they feel some guilt. They corrupted me and got off without punishment whilst I was forced to marry an old man."

The viscount sat back. "Do you expect me to feel sorry for you, my dear? It is the way of the world and you know it. You knew it when you allowed the twins to touch you when you were but eighteen and you knew it when you allowed them to touch you now."

I sucked in a breath and continued to gaze at him. He shook his head. "We stray from the point. Gervase insists he wants to marry you to make up for your years of torment, his words not mine, with Mr. Carstairs. Has he mentioned marriage to you?"

I shook my head, pride insisting that I stay upright in my chair and look my accuser in the eye.

"I wonder why not?" The viscount mused. "Maybe you have been foolish, Eden, and allowed him the freedom of your body without extracting any promises from him." He shrugged his elegant shoulders. "Why should Gervase bother to marry you when he has already had you?"

The deliberate crudity from a man who scarcely needed to use such language set my teeth on edge. I struggled to remember that it was not as he believed.

"No, my lord, Gervase has not offered me marriage, nor did I expect him to. I chose to share my body with him." I cocked an insolent eyebrow at the viscount who sat back as if amused. "Does it shock you that a woman might have needs like a man?"

The viscount smiled. "Nothing shocks me, my dear. I offer you my congratulations. Not many women in your position would be brave enough to turn down an offer of marriage. Not even one made out of pity. And make no mistake, what Gervase feels for you is guilt and pity." His eyes narrowed to the color of flint and he leaned slightly towards me.

"Let us take the gloves off and discuss this matter properly. I do not wish Gervase to marry you but not for the reasons you might imagine." He must have sensed my bewilderment as he smiled again. "You are a beautiful and sensual woman. A woman who reminds me greatly of the twins' mother."

He folded his hands together on the desk and looked down at them. "I do not say that lightly. Louisa was the light of my life and if I were but twenty years younger I suspect I would be brawling over you myself." His mouth twisted. "But as I grow older and more aware of the fragility of life I have a strange desire to see my line established."

My stomach ceased to burn with nerves and instead seemed to fill with ashes as the viscount captured my gaze. "I want grandchildren, Eden. Gideon's wife is unstable, and God forbid I should wish harm on her, but Gideon swears he will not lie with her even to make a child." He sighed. "And that leaves Gervase."

His voice softened and I tensed my shoulders to repel his apparent sympathy. "You were married for several years to a man who was desperate for a child. He swore to me he would bed you every night until you gave him one."

He sat back. "You didn't conceive, my dear, and I cannot allow you to marry my son and threaten my chances for grandchildren. Gervase deserves children. He would be an excellent father. He might tell you that it doesn't matter to him but I suspect you know that for a virile man like Gervase it does."

The room blurred before my eyes. I realized that I had been weeping for a while as I listened to the viscount. He knew I was but a barren shell. He was right. I couldn't deprive Gervase of the chance of children. I fought for control as the silence lengthened, marred only by the ticking of the mantel clock. At length, an elegant hand appeared at my elbow and dropped a large handkerchief into my lap.

I drew in several slow breaths, blew my nose and lifted my head to find the viscount watching me.

"You may rest easy, my lord," I whispered. "I never intended to entrap Gervase. I wished only to enjoy my widowhood for a short while until you found another elderly husband to stifle me with."

The viscount met my gaze, a hint of respect and understanding in there which nearly made me cry again. He glanced down at a list of names on his desk.

"As to that, they are not all elderly," he said gently. "Some are even men with young families to raise who would love the care of a new mother."

I gathered my courage. "If I accept what you say about Gervase, will you allow me some element of choice this time?"

The viscount folded the piece of paper and handed it to me with a wave of his hand. "Of course. I would have allowed that anyway." He hesitated. "And time to make that choice if you so desire it."

I nodded and he passed another heavier package across the desk to me. "I have made arrangements for you to reside at this cottage on my estate near Brighton. All the men on your list will come and visit with you, at your invitation, over the summer. Perhaps by Christmas you will have made your decision?"

I stowed the bulky papers away in my reticule and knew that when I left Harcourt House I would be escorted with considerable speed and every luxury to my new home. I drew in a hard-won breath.

"I don't think I can face Gervase again." I tried to laugh but my voice shook. "How can I ask him if he wishes to marry me and then decline his offer all in one breath? Can you give him my apologies?"

The viscount bowed. "Of course. I would not expect you to deliver such news in person."

I got to my feet, suddenly desperate to be away from all the Harcourts and their compelling charm. When I reached the door, the viscount asked, "You love him, don't you?"

I turned to face him. "Yes, too much to saddle him with a barren wife."

He released his breath with a gentle sigh. "Godspeed then, Eden, and thank you for your understanding."

I stepped out into the brightness of Hanover Square and made my way to the discreet closed carriage that awaited me. I smiled at the footman who assisted me into the carriage and slammed the door. A sharp pain under my ribs made me breathless and I had to suck in great gulps of air. I wrapped my arms around myself and allowed the sway of the carriage to rock me. Tears came and my heart shattered into a thousand pieces as I drew further and further away from Gervase.

Chapter Eight

ॐ

I swore in an extremely unladylike manner as a closed carriage swept past and doused me in filthy, muddy rainwater. Two months had passed since my flight from London. I glared up at the sky. It was supposed to be summer. The changeable weather suited my troubled mind. When I set out to walk to the vicarage the weather was mild and the skies clear. Now, as the heavens opened, I regretted not accepting the vicar's offer of a ride home in his carriage. At the time it had seemed pointless to expect him to harness his horses for a journey of less than ten minutes. Now as sullen rain filled clouds gathered in ever darkening ranks, I hurried to find my way home.

At last, I ran up my flower-lined path, head lowered against the buffeting wind and straight into the hall calling for my maid. There was no reply as I shook out my sodden cloak and kicked my ruined kid slippers aside. A welcome light in the best parlor beckoned me through the darkness. I entered the room and struggled with the ties of my bonnet.

My fingers stilled on the doorknob as I took in a pair of muddy army boots planted on my hearth. I slowly looked upwards. Gervase stood with his back to the small fire absorbing all the heat. In the confines of my thatched cottage, his rain-dampened hair brushed the oak beams that crossed the white plastered ceiling.

"I sent your maid home."

I could only stare at him like a simpleton as I tried to see his face from beneath my dripping bonnet. He looked desperately tired. Shadows made harsh purple streaks under his eyes and he was unshaven. My fingers itched to smooth the furrowed lines from his brow. I remained frozen to the spot.

With a final tug, the ribbons of my bonnet snapped. I pulled the sodden confection from my head and looked around the neat, well-ordered room for a place to deposit it. Gervase seemed to have taken up all the space and all the available air. I took two hasty steps backwards.

"I will go and make some tea." I gestured to my bonnet. "And find somewhere to hang this. Excuse me for a moment."

I escaped into the kitchen where my maid, Katie, had left a good fire burning. My teeth chattered as I struggled to locate the teapot and the necessary items for the promised cup of tea.

"Your hair is wet."

I spun around with a gasp as Gervase tossed a cloth at me and gestured to my head. With murmured thanks, I went across to the fire and sank down onto my knees. I started to unpin my hair then thought better of it as I sensed Gervase come up behind me. I patted my fringe and side curls into some semblance of order and turned to make the tea as the kettle hissed to the boil.

Gervase waited by the door until I had the tray ready. He picked it up without a word and carried it through to the parlor. He built up the fire as I lit more lamps and closed the velvet curtains against the miserable gray skies.

At first I could do little more than sip my tea and enjoy the warmth of the fire. I sought desperately for something to say to Gervase. I hadn't seen him for two months. His reappearance in my life was so unexpected yet so secretly longed for that I had to pinch myself to make sure I hadn't conjured him out of my fevered imagination.

As I pondered what to say, Gervase broke the silence.

"Are you not curious as to how I found you, Eden?"

I could only nod, a polite smile on my lips.

"I wasted over a week searching for you in Glasgow without any help from your husband's family. When I returned, your mother was most helpful in securing your direction after my father swore he could not aid me." His mouth tightened. "It didn't occur to me that you might hide right under my bloody nose on my own father's estate."

I offered him some milk for his tea. He declined with a shudder. "Wherever did you go on such an unpleasant day and why the hell didn't you take your maid?"

I bristled at his abrasive tone. "I only went to the village church to help with the flowers." I had no intention of revealing that I went there most days to pray for his safety. "I was invited to lunch at the vicarage. I walked home from there."

Gervase's frown deepened and he opened his mouth. I quickly spoke over him. "The vicar did offer me the use of his carriage but it scarce seemed worth the wait when I could walk home in ten minutes."

Gervase growled. "How old is this vicar?"

I lifted the teapot to refill my cup and directed a blistering stare at my tormentor over the top of it.

"I am not one of your new recruits, Major Harcourt. You have no right to interrogate me."

Gervase crossed one booted foot over the other and stretched out his legs until he deliberately brushed my skirts.

"So he's young then." His eyes lowered to my bodice. "I am surprised that he did not offer to walk you home in the rain. He would have enjoyed the view."

I followed his gaze downward to my soaked bodice, which clung to every curve of my breasts and clearly displayed my nipples. Gervase tutted and shook his head. "Still no proper corset, I see. Are you disappointed that he didn't escort you?"

He leaned forward to pour himself another cup of tea and drank it down in one swallow. I attempted to pull the fabric of my gown into a more modest position.

Gervase gave a dry laugh. "Don't bother on my account. I've been hard since you walked into the house."

I gave up the attempt to cover myself and sat back in my chair, watching Gervase with all the caution of a mouse cornered by a tomcat.

"What I would really like to know, Eden, is whether my father was right. He insists you never intended to marry me, that you were using me for your own sexual gratification whilst you waited for the right man to come along." He placed his cup with great precision into its saucer and stared at me. "Well?"

I cradled my cup, glad I had something to hold onto. "I am sorry if my answer disappoints you, but your father is right. That was my intent."

"I don't believe you."

I stood up and banged my cup down on the table. "Why not? Do you think you are so irresistible? I don't recall you asking me to marry you or stay with you. You seemed more than content to take what I offered without any promises. The only reason you have hunted me down now is hurt pride."

"Christ, no!" He dragged his hand through his curling hair and glared right back at me. "I came because I wanted to talk to you, because you left me so abruptly and because..." he hesitated. "Because I wanted to see you again before I leave for France."

A glut of tears threatened to choke me as I heard the concern in his voice. I turned abruptly away.

"I notice that you did not come to inquire if I were breeding." I clenched my fists. "Well, surprise, surprise, I am not."

Gervase gave a quiet laugh. "Ah...so that's how he did it. The clever old bastard."

I turned in confusion as he advanced towards me, the smile lingering on his lips.

"I have just realized how my devious father persuaded you to abandon me again. He used your fear of being barren." He held out his hand. "What else did he say? Some drivel about wanting grandchildren?" He snorted. "He has a daughter, you know, and I do not see Gideon's wife enjoying a long life if she continues to pursue her current obsessions."

Horrified by my own stupidity, I tried to push past him. He caught my elbow and I had to stop.

"I told you why I left, Gervase. You were just available to me when I needed a man. There is no more to be said."

"You are lying."

I raised my hand to strike him. He captured my wrists and dragged both of my arms behind my back. He easily encircled my wrists with one hand. I tried to calm my breathing as Gervase urged me even closer. My breasts brushed his chest, tightening my nipples every time I inhaled.

"Most men would love to have a woman who doesn't want anything from them except sex," I said wildly. "Why can't you accept that it's over?"

"Because it's not." Gervase spat out the words as I struggled against him. "I wanted to ask you to marry me the first moment I saw you again but you didn't seem to want anything from me but sex. At first, I tried to pretend that that was all I wanted from you too, but my heart knew better." His voice gentled. "Can you imagine how I felt when the chance to amend for my past mistakes fell into my lap and you seemed happy to forgive me?"

I brought my chin up and stared into his intent blue eyes. "You are lying now, Gervase. You never spoke of love, only of lust."

He gave a strangled laugh. "Eden, give me some credit. No self-respecting nineteen-year-old boy would have spent a whole day preparing you to take him inside you without loving you. Every other woman I touched at that age was lucky to get more than five minutes of self-indulgent sex from me. You were always different. You were always special. It was always love."

I wanted so desperately to believe him. I gave in to the temptation to rest my forehead against his embroidered waistcoat and then summoned all my strength to push him away.

"Go away, Gervase. I do not want this."

He caught and held my fingers. "I am only going to ask you this once," he said abruptly. "Will you marry me?"

I shook my head and refused to meet his eyes. His fingers settled under my chin and forced me to look up at him. Still holding my gaze, he reached into his pocket and produced a crumpled piece of parchment. I tried to snatch it from his grasp. He held it at a safe distance.

"Where did you get that from?" I cried. "It belongs to me."

"I found it while I waited for you to return."

Gervase opened the parchment with a disdainful flick of his wrist. "This is, I presume, a list of potential husbands supplied to you by my father?"

I could only stare at him, my lips firmly shut, and watch the anger build in his suddenly arctic blue eyes. With a muttered oath, he released me and crossed to my desk. He plucked my quill from its inkstand and spread the parchment out onto the blotter. I clenched my teeth as the pen screeched and scratched across the face of the list. He held my gaze as he held the parchment aloft. Ink slid and dripped onto the carpet. Despite the mess, I could clearly read his flamboyant signature scrawled over the other names.

"Does this make it clear to you?" He spoke through his teeth. "If you marry anyone, it will be me."

I backed away from him, one eye on the door.

"You are no gentleman, sir. If you were, you would take your answer and leave me in peace."

He leapt for me as I attempted to flee. I found myself pinned against the door.

"You are right," he said almost soundlessly, the soft hiss of his breath warm against my throat. "I am no gentleman. I have a special license in my pocket. You'll marry me tomorrow in London in front of my father and Gideon and then you'll accompany me to France."

I struggled to breathe and his arms relaxed a fraction of an inch.

"You'll stay close to me until I go into action and you'll sleep alongside me wherever I tell you to." His tone grew harsher and he fought to pull up my skirts. "I'll want to make love to you all the time. When you are my wife I'll take you whenever I want to." He ripped off my undergarments and threw them to the floor. "You'll forget what it's like not to have my cock inside you and you'll want it as much as me." He braced me against the door and tore open his breeches. His penetration was fast and rough and drove me against the door.

I gasped as he pressed deeper and harder, and gloried in the feel of him and the sense of completion. With a sob, my hand curled into the crisp golden hair at the nape of his neck. He shuddered.

"This is how it will be from now on, Eden. I'll be inside you whenever I can and you'll not refuse me whether we're surrounded by the whole of Wellington's army or in the middle of a dinner party." With each word, he thrust deeper and deeper. "Some days, I'll not let you out of bed at all and you'll lie there naked and wet from my seed just waiting for me to fill you again."

He increased his pace and I locked my heels in the small of his back to hold him inside me for as long as possible. I screamed into his warm generous mouth as I came. He followed me with a final bucking of his hips as he strove to drive even deeper. As I collapsed against his shoulder, he put his hand around my ankles and held me locked against him.

He smoothed the tangled hair from my face and looked down at me, his voice gentle and hoarse.

"I told you that I'd not ask you again, but you will marry me. I might be killed in this battle and my father's dynastic ambitions mean nothing to me." He cleared his throat and pressed on. "I want you with me as my wife. I do not care if we have a child. I just want you."

I kissed his mouth and his face lightened. He wiped the tears from my cheeks with fingers that shook and began to smile.

"I forgot to mention, in my passion, that the same rules apply to you too, love. Whenever you want me. I am yours."

His simple words conjured up a thousand enticing prospects for sensual mischief. I smiled back at him.

"Whenever I want you?" I asked. A hint of caution entered Gervase's blue eyes and he nodded. I squeezed my heels hard into the small of his back and felt his cock jump inside me. I caught his bottom lip between my teeth and bit down with exquisite care.

"How about now?" I whispered as his tongue thrust into my mouth and stopped me from speaking. Then he pulled back. His blue eyes searched mine, his expression vulnerable.

"Only if you tell me that you love me. Only if you want to make love and not just have sex."

I kissed him full on the lips and wound my arms around his neck. "Oh, I love you, Gervase," I murmured against his mouth. "Love me back…"

ANTONIA'S BARGAIN

છ૰

Chapter One
London, 1816

ю

"Who is that?"

Lord Gideon Harcourt studied the young gentleman who stood by the fireplace in the salon of Madame Desiree's House of Pleasure. The man's gaze remained fixed on the fireplace as if he was oblivious or impervious to the riotous pursuit of sexual gratification going on around him.

Madame Desiree shrugged. "I'm not sure of his name. I believe he came in with Lady Jane Mellows." She pursed her lips. "He does seem a mite uncomfortable and he looks rather young. Do you think I should send him home?"

"With his tail between his legs?"

Gideon smiled at Madame Desiree. For a woman who ran a house unsurpassed for the level of erotic fantasies offered for the amusement of the rich, she was remarkably sentimental. He kissed her hand.

"Don't worry, cherie, I will take care of him for you."

She laughed and rapped his knuckles with her fan. "Be nice, Gideon."

He winked at her. "When am I ever anything but?"

To the young man's left, two women played a game of cards, which involved the loser removing items of clothing. Shrieks of laughter wafted over to Gideon as one of the ladies tore off a stocking and flung it straight toward the fire.

He concealed a smile as he reached his prey. It took him but a moment to untangle the hapless youth from the still warm silk stocking that landed on his face. The young man gave him a relieved grin.

"Thanks for your help, sir. For a moment I feared I had gone blind."

"There are far better ways to go blind, my dear boy, particularly here." Gideon gestured at the crowded room. "Is this your first visit to Madame Desiree's?"

"Indeed it is." The youth tugged at his badly tied cravat. "Is it that obvious?"

Gideon guided him toward the buffet table. "To a man as experienced as I am, yes." He handed him a glass of champagne. "Am I permitted to know your name?"

A flash of guilt crossed the boy's pleasant features. "Of course, sir, I am Anthony, erm, Smith."

Gideon raised an eyebrow. "It's remarkable how many of the patrons of this elegant and discreet establishment go by the name of Smith. You must meet a lot of relatives." He bowed. "I'm Harcourt. Lord Gideon Harcourt."

Anthony studied him with wide gray eyes. They reminded Gideon of a deep lake on a calm day. How old was the boy? A shiver of heightened awareness coursed down his spine. Anthony's skin was as smooth as the finest porcelain. Gideon's fingers itched to trace the curve of his high cheekbones.

"Did you come here by yourself tonight?"

He gestured to a chair and took the one opposite. Anthony crossed one long leg over the other and finished off the champagne. "No, my lord. I came with a connection of mine." He leaned forward, the flush on his cheeks rising. "In truth, I didn't know quite what I was letting myself in for."

Around them swelled the intimate sounds of subdued music, foreplay and lovemaking. The unmistakable scent of arousal mingled with candle wax and heated, perfumed bodies. Gideon paused to admire the tangle of limbs on the couch to his left where three women and a single man seemed to be convulsing in simultaneous orgasm.

He'd had the dubious pleasure of fornicating with two of the women earlier in the evening. One of them was a duchess, the other her sister. He had good reason to know their sexual appetites were voracious. Not that he intended to bed them again. He rarely found anything interesting enough in a partner of either sex to warrant a repeat performance. He noticed that Anthony kept his gaze on the badly polished toecaps of his boots.

An unwilling laugh shook through him. Had he ever been that naïve? He and his identical twin, Gervase, had learned to pleasure women as soon as they'd developed the ability to get an erection. Damnation, he missed his twin. Would the cursed aftermath of the war with France never end?

And why was this youth so inexperienced? Gideon's keen gaze dropped to Anthony's long, narrow hands, noted the ill-fitting cut of his breeches and lingered there. He drew in a slow breath and savored his interesting discovery, more aroused than before.

"It's true that Madame Desiree caters to some unusual tastes. Do you find lovemaking offensive?"

Anthony raised his fine eyes to Gideon's. "No, it's just that I've never seen…" He waved his hand helplessly in the general direction of the women.

"Ah, I begin to understand you. You believe that women are not meant to enjoy the act of physical love, only men."

He met a fiery glare that surprised him. The boy had spirit. He felt more interested and alive than he had in months.

"On the contrary, why should women not enjoy themselves?" He glanced around the room. "But in public?"

Gideon snapped his fingers and one of the footmen refilled their glasses. "This is scarcely public. Madame Desiree presides over the most discreet and expensive club in the city. Perhaps you should start your sexual education in a more traditional setting."

Anthony frowned. "What do you mean?"

"There are several tried and tested routes." Anthony's cheeks grew even redder. "Some fathers take their sons to their own mistresses for their first lessons in the carnal arts."

"That's obscene. Why would any man want to share his father's mistress?"

Gideon was beginning to enjoy himself. He drank his champagne in one swallow. "Perhaps you feel this way because your father was unwilling to share?"

"My father didn't have a mistress, he…"

Gideon held his gaze. "Are you sure about that?" Anthony was the first to look away.

"As I was saying, another traditional route to the joys of fornication is to find a young woman in your parents' employ who is willing to oblige you."

Anthony compressed his lips into a thin line. "And what happens to the woman if she becomes pregnant? From what I've heard, she would be thrown out of the house to starve."

"Are you perhaps a Puritan or a Methodist, Anthony? You sound so disapproving."

"I am neither, sir. It just seems unfair."

Gideon drew a cigar from his pocket and offered one to Anthony who shook his head. He took his time lighting his, allowed the smoke to weave a screen around him and his silent companion.

"The third option, of course, is the traditional brothel. As long as you can find somewhere discreet, clean and safe, you are guaranteed anonymity. You pay for the woman's services, you use her body and then you leave." He smiled into Anthony's outraged eyes. "Surely you can have no objections to that?"

To his amusement, Anthony remained close-mouthed. Gideon resisted an urge to lean forward and run a thumb over his generous lower lip.

"Have I embarrassed you?"

Anthony let out a breath. "No indeed, sir, you have just confirmed my intolerable ignorance about the ways of the flesh."

Gideon drew on his cigar, aware of a slight hardening and heat in his groin as Anthony uncrossed and then recrossed his long legs.

"Where have you been for all these years? In a monastery?"

"I might as well have been!" Indignation threaded through his clipped words. "I've been kept in the country, sheltered and overprotected and then expected to marry some stupid—" He closed his mouth with a snap. "I apologize, sir. My indignation got the better of me."

Gideon shifted in his seat as his cock hardened. "Are you saying your family intends to force you into a marriage while you are still a virgin?"

"That is why I begged—I mean, asked—Lady Jane to bring me here tonight. I thought I should be allowed to understand what went on for myself."

"And Lady Jane refused to initiate you? How vexing of her."

"She is my cousin. I hardly think she would want to do that."

Gideon winked at him. "You'd be surprised what goes on in the best of families."

"But I want to find out for myself," Anthony repeated, his face set in a stubborn expression that reminded Gideon of his father.

"An excellent plan." He got to his feet. "If it pleases you, I will consider myself your guide tonight. I promise to answer any questions you might have."

Anthony rose too, his expression wary. "Why would you do this for me, sir?"

"Because I am bored and you promise to provide me with a great deal of amusement."

"What if Lady Jane should need me?"

Gideon took the glass out of Anthony's hand and steered him toward the door. His young protégé obviously hadn't noticed that Lady Jane was one of the women writhing on the couch in front of them. "I doubt she will, but I will make sure she knows where to find you."

As they walked down the long carpeted corridor, he admired Anthony's profile and his disheveled brown hair styled a la Brutus. Gideon reckoned Anthony was about five-feet nine-inches tall. Five inches shorter than him. Mentally reviewing the many scandalous delights on offer at Madame Desiree's, Gideon stopped at the fifth door on the left. A plaque on the door read Fairy Tales.

"Here would be a good place to start."

He opened the door and stood back to allow Anthony to precede him. To his delight the room was dark and almost deserted. He followed Anthony to an empty row of chairs and sat beside him. As they settled in their seats, a footman appeared and began to light a set of candles in a large circle in the center of the room. Light illuminated the shadow of a painted tree and the patch of fake grass beneath it.

Gideon stretched his left arm along the back of Anthony's chair and brought his mouth close to the boy's ear. He slowly inhaled. Anthony smelled of lavender soap and innocence, something Gideon had begun to believe no longer existed. "I think you will enjoy this. It's a tale about the power of lust."

A young man dressed in medieval clothing came into the circle of light. In his hands he held a lute which he began to strum. A second, unseen player added a mournful counter-melody that was followed by the soft beat of a drum. A woman stepped out of the shadows. Anthony jerked upright, his back making contact with Gideon's arm. He didn't move away.

The woman wore a transparent white gown. Her long blonde hair hung to her knees and was crowned by a garland of flowers and precious gems. The thin fabric did nothing to conceal the dark hue of her nipples or the triangle of hair at the apex of her thighs.

Anthony let out a breath. "The Queen of the Fairies and Thomas the Rhymer."

Gideon allowed his fingertips to drop onto Anthony's shoulder. "Despite your youth, I see you are well-educated."

On the stage, Thomas sat down under the tree and continued to strum his lute as if oblivious to the vision beside him. The Fairy Queen knelt in front of him and kissed his cheek. Still Thomas played on.

"What exactly am I supposed to learn from this, sir? It's a fairy tale," Anthony whispered. To Gideon's delight, he sounded slightly shaken.

"Watch and see. I'll ask you again afterwards." He stretched out his fingers, felt the fast beat of Anthony's pulse at the base of his skull.

The Fairy Queen brought her hands to her breasts and cupped them as if offering them to Thomas. For the first time his fingers faltered on the lute. She circled her nipples with her thumbs until they stood out proudly through her dress. Leaning forward, she brushed one taut nipple across Thomas' lips. He sucked her nipple into his mouth and held it there, pulling strongly on her.

Anthony swallowed hard, his body tensing under Gideon's light touch. "Is that pleasurable for a woman? To be suckled by a man as if he is her babe?"

In the darkness Gideon smiled at the curiosity in his voice. "Aye, pleasurable for both. You would enjoy it immensely. Personally, I enjoy suckling a woman with smaller breasts. There is less to suffocate in."

Anthony stifled a choke of laughter. "I've never thought of it like that."

"Men are sensitive there too. I enjoy a lover's mouth on me."

Gideon's cock throbbed as Anthony's startled gaze lowered to his chest. Hell's teeth, at this moment he'd settle for a nip on any part of his body.

Anthony swiveled back in his seat as if stuck with a pin. Had he seen something in Gideon's expression that unsettled him? Gideon hoped so.

On the stage, the Fairy Queen was determined to attract the mortal Thomas' interest. When he continued to play, she stripped off her gown and sat cross-legged in front of him. She licked her middle finger and placed it between her legs.

Anthony whispered in his ear, the sound a mere thread. "What is she doing?"

"I believe she has decided to play with herself if Thomas will not oblige her." A devil of mischief made him continue. "You cannot be so innocent that you have never touched yourself?"

"No, I mean, yes, of course I have…"

Gideon cupped his own growing erection and squeezed. He wasn't sure which intrigued him most. The sights on the stage or the sight of Anthony trying to pretend he wasn't excited.

The Fairy Queen slid her fingers in and out of her sheath; the wetness on her skin caught the light of the candles. With her other hand she rolled and pinched her nipples. She swayed in time with the music, toward and away from Thomas.

The rhythm of the music grew more insistent. Thomas grabbed the Fairy Queen's hand from her breast and pressed it to his groin before resuming his playing. She untied his laces to reveal his engorged shaft. Gideon stroked his own cock as he measured the width and breadth of the other man's erection. Bigger than most, but not as big as his.

Beside him, Anthony shivered and brought his hand up to cover his mouth. As the Fairy Queen bent to take Thomas' cock between her teeth, Thomas' fingers fell away from the strings. With a groan, he cast aside his lute and reached for her. She gasped as he pulled her head back and kissed her mouth.

Anthony made a stifled sound as Thomas then slid down the woman's body and licked the woman's sex. The beat of the drum resonated through the room as the couple fell into a frantic embrace. With a muttered excuse, Anthony shot to his feet and headed for the door.

Within five strides, Gideon caught up with him and took hold of his arm.

"Let me go, sir." Anthony's cheeks were flushed, his pupils dilated.

Gideon tightened his grip. "I think we need to talk." He pushed Anthony into one of the deserted bedchambers and shut the door. He took his time lighting the candles and kindling a fire in the grate. The candlelight revealed red silk walls and thick velvet bed hangings that suited his mood. He wondered how the velvet would feel against his cock, against the soft cream of Anthony's skin. After a swift glance at his captive, he poured himself a brandy from the tray on the dresser.

Anthony remained by the door, his hands thrust into his pockets.

"Why did you run away?"

"I didn't run. I just felt I had seen enough."

"You found the scene offensive?"

Anthony simply stared at him. Gideon put down his glass and moved closer. "Perhaps that isn't it. Perhaps you found it arousing and you simply couldn't allow yourself to be human and enjoy it."

"That's not true. It was disgusting, it was…"

Gideon stopped in front of him. "It was sex. Isn't that what you wanted to find out about?"

Anthony's chest rose and fell in agitation. "Maybe that's why we are supposed to wait until the privacy of a marriage bed. Maybe these acts are too intimate to be displayed for an audience."

"Ah, I see. A coward as well as a liar."

Gideon grabbed Anthony's hand and pressed it to the front of his breeches. "I am aroused. Watching them couple and watching you watching them made me hard."

"How dare you!"

Anthony wrenched his hand away and turned to the door. Gideon braced his palm against it to prevent escape. He deliberately used his superior weight to keep Anthony against the door, pressing his erection against those exquisitely slim buttocks.

He brought his hand around and cupped Anthony between the legs.

"Now if I were truly a gentleman I would agree that you do not appear to be aroused. Your cock is in fact, nonexistent. I could be charitable and assume that the reason for your lack of balls is due to a tragic accident or an unfortunate castration."

Anthony tried to push away but Gideon held fast. "But you are aroused."

With easy strength, he turned Anthony to face him. He ran his fingers over the front of her coat. "Are your nipples tight and hard under your waistcoat? Do you find the bindings chafe against your tender flesh?"

He brought his hand to her face and touched her cheek. "Your skin is flushed and your eyes are wide with excitement whether you want them to be or not." She tried to speak but seemed unable to form the words. Gideon smiled as he recaptured her mound. "And although you have no cock to betray you, I can smell your desire." He pressed his middle finger hard against the seam of her breeches. "I'll wager you are wet and ready for sex down here."

She tried to kick him. He dragged her into an even closer embrace, more sexually excited than he'd been for years. He threaded his fingers into her hair and made her look at him. To his delight, passion mingled with anger in her direct stare. He rocked his hips, allowed her to feel the length and heat of his shaft against her belly.

"Are you going to force me?"

"I've never taken a woman who wasn't willing."

She swallowed hard. "Well then, do you intend to expose me as a fraud?"

Gideon raised an eyebrow. "Why would I wish to do that? You didn't deceive me for more than five minutes."

"So you have been playing with me all along."

"I have been humoring you. And in a way, protecting you from others less scrupulous than myself. Madame Desiree's is no place for an inexperienced woman."

She shifted her stance and Gideon fought a groan.

"Will you let me go and find my companion then?"

Unable to resist her bold courage, he stepped back. "Of course, my dear. But may I suggest you go straight home?"

Her breasts rose and fell with each agitated breath. "Did you do this to punish me? Did I amuse you?"

Gideon glanced down at his erect cock which fought the confines of his breeches. "You did much more than that."

Her gaze followed his and fixed on the outline of his shaft. She seemed unable to look away.

"Why do I feel as if I am being allowed to leave too easily?"

Gideon bowed. "If you truly wish to learn how to be a gentleman, come back here in a week. I promise to teach you all you need to know."

He reached into his coat pocket and extracted a card. He pressed it into her hand and opened the door. "Goodnight, Anthony, sweet dreams."

He watched her walk down the corridor and then shut the door. Absentmindedly he helped himself to another brandy. For the first time since his wife's suicide, he felt truly alive. After her death, he'd drowned his guilt and rage in an orgy of drunkenness and sex. Only his twin's refusal to let him waste his life had saved him from the abyss of self-pity. Wincing slightly, he unbuttoned his breeches and released his cock. Should he call for assistance or manage by himself? He rang the bell.

Seating himself by the fire, Gideon wrapped his hand around the base of his shaft. Damnation, he should have asked Anthony what her real name was. Her soft accent had held a hint of Wales. He imagined her fingering her hard nipples, maybe thinking about him and the sights he had shown her. He groaned and rested his head against the back of the chair. In his vast and varied sexual experience it was rare for a woman to hold his attention. But Anthony had.

In truth, when he'd realized Anthony was a woman, he'd been almost relieved. Such a sudden, intense attraction to a man had never happened to him before. He frowned down at his cock. Perhaps he should be more concerned. The last time he'd felt this interested in a woman he'd ended up married and in a relationship from hell.

The door to the bedchamber opened and a man and a woman dressed in Madame Desiree's discreet uniform appeared. He studied them as they came to kneel on either side of him. Did he want the quick coarseness of a man's mouth or the slow seductiveness of a woman's?

He wanted both.

At his command, the servants bent to their task, taking turns to pleasure his cock. Gideon shut his eyes as he neared completion and concentrated on Anthony's deep gray eyes. At first, her body language had confused him. She moved as freely and confidently as a man and had made no effort to appear womanly even when he confronted her. Perhaps that was part of her appeal. The outward traits of a man concealing the soft, stimulating curves of a woman's body.

Would she have the nerve to return and take him up on his provocative offer? To his surprise his discovery that Anthony was a woman hadn't depleted his lust, only exacerbated it. He devoutly hoped she would come back.

He groaned as the female servant gripped his balls and sucked his shaft. He eased her mouth away and beckoned to the man. Hard and fast and rough now until his come left his aching balls and traveled up his shaft to pour into the welcoming wet cavern of the servant's mouth. The woman kissed his thigh, her fingers digging into his buttocks through his breeches. He stroked her long black hair, wondered how Anthony's short curls would feel under his hand. For the first time in a long while his future seemed open to endless possibilities.

"Anthony? Are you ready to leave?"

Lady Jane stood in the doorway to the main salon and beckoned imperiously to Antonia. With a last, hasty glance down the corridor, she straightened her cravat and sauntered across to her cousin. Jane's cheeks were flushed, her eyes bright. For the first time, Antonia realized exactly why her cousin was so invigorated.

"Are you ready to go, my lady?" She swept Jane a bow and gladly placed a hand on her sleeve. "In truth, I have seen enough and I am eager for my bed."

Jane glanced at her and winked. "Mr. Maxwell. Did you not find something interesting to do to pass the time?"

An image of Lord Gideon Harcourt's patrician features flashed across Antonia's mind. "Alas, no. I did exactly as you told me and stayed put in the main salon."

Jane pinched her. "Then where were you when I looked for you?"

Antonia grinned as she assisted Jane into their carriage.

"I was right there, Janey. The question is where were you? And exactly what were you doing in such an appalling place?"

Jane flushed as she settled her skirts on the seat. "It is not an appalling place. It is the height of fashion. And even you must guess why I go there. My dear husband is seventy. I'm only thirty. He can no longer offer me any bed sport and I need it."

Antonia frowned at her cousin. "All I saw were a large number of scantily dressed persons of quality behaving inappropriately in a public setting."

"La! Antonia, you sound more like our grandmother every day." Jane fanned herself vigorously. "Just because you choose to behave like a Puritan, do not expect everyone else to."

"I'm sorry, coz." Antonia leaned forward and patted Jane's knee. "I know your life is not easy. It was just a shock to see…"

"People enjoying themselves?" Jane didn't seem to be mollified.

Antonia sighed. She had been in London for three weeks and its customs and loose morals still bewildered her. Perhaps Jane was right and she had become a fussy old maid. At twenty-six she believed she was long past the age to dream of marriage and a family. But it seemed that fate, in the shape of her grandmother and cousin Charles, had decreed otherwise.

"It was a fascinating experience, Jane, and I thank you for allowing me to accompany you."

Jane glared at her over the top of her fan. "You said that you wanted to understand my life. You said you were bored being a provincial nobody."

Antonia winced. "I didn't quite put it like that, but yes, I did say I wanted to try new things." She smoothed her cravat. "And I always enjoy dressing as a man." She remembered the press of Gideon Harcourt's legs against hers, the way he'd cupped her mound and rubbed his fingers against her heat.

112

The carriage stopped and Antonia waited for the footman to let down the steps. She helped Jane out and escorted her inside. After wishing her cousin goodnight, she took herself off to her bedroom. With a sigh, she slipped off the coat and shirt Jane had borrowed from her husband's wardrobe.

In the mirror, the white linen that bound her breasts made her skin look even paler. She slowly unwound the bandage. Gideon was right, her nipples were hard. With one trembling finger, she touched one taut pink peak. How would a man's mouth feel on her? She closed her eyes and imagined clutching handfuls of Gideon's golden hair as she pressed his mouth to her breast.

She opened her breeches and slid her fingers inside to caress her sex. Unaccustomed heat swelled in her belly and she opened her legs a little wider to allow her fingers more room to work. Gideon was so tall he had overwhelmed her completely, handled her body with an ease and assurance that should have made her feel helpless but had invigorated her. Pressure built as she rubbed herself until it became unbearable. Frustration at her failure to ever find completion diluted her passion and made her want to scream.

Did she dare meet Gideon again? She opened her eyes and stared at her reflection. In the mirror she looked as wanton as the Fairy Queen as she had sucked her lover's cock. With a shudder, Antonia removed the rest of her clothing and dressed in a demure white nightgown. She climbed into bed. Her solitary life in rural Wales had shielded her from temptation for too long.

Until she'd told Gideon Harcourt about her sexual ignorance, she hadn't realized how angry she felt about her family's ambitions to marry her off. None of them had expected her to be left such a large personal legacy from her grandmother. Before that, they'd been quite content to leave her moldering in the old manor house acting as her grandmother's sole companion and nurse. Now everything had changed and her cousin Charles intended her to wed a man who could help further his political ambitions.

She recalled Gideon's bold offer. Her London cousins didn't know her very well. Despite her serene appearance, her upbringing had scarcely been conventional. Her widowed father had let her run wild and she'd been ignored by her grandmother until she became too frail to care for herself. She'd spent half her life dressed in breeches. It was difficult for her to remember that women were supposed to act as if they were frail and needed a man's support. Would Gideon really allow her to experience the unknown, intriguing world of a *tonnish* gentleman? It would be an excellent way to discover how the men who aspired to her hand behaved without their womenfolk around them.

Antonia shivered and curled up into a tight ball. She wasn't prepared to play the dutiful unmarried innocent. She had her own money and deserved to decide exactly what her marriage would entail before she entered into it. In truth, if she could not find a suitable gentleman to agree to her proposal, she hoped to avoid it all together. If all her female relations, except Jane, chose to remain tight-lipped about the marriage-bed, she would find out for herself. She sighed into the frigid air. Perhaps with a little help from a tall elegant man with a dangerous smile.

Chapter Two
ॐ

"Sir, I am not trying to be difficult."

Gideon tried to unclench his jaw as his father, Viscount Harcourt DeVere, paced the narrow strip of carpet behind his desk. It was difficult not to feel like a child again when the study brought back so many memories, most of them unpleasant. If he looked closely, the front trim of the mahogany desk still bore the indentations of his fingernails where he'd been bent over to receive a particularly severe beating.

"You have made no effort to find a new wife."

"Caroline has only been dead a year. I hardly think that is a long time."

His father snorted. "Don't try and pretend you are still in mourning for her."

"A year of mourning is considered customary these days. She was a troubled woman, Father. And in truth, I regret her passing."

His father halted, hands clasped behind his back. "Why? She was no credit to you."

Gideon drew a deep steadying breath. "Caroline found life very difficult. I wish I could have done more to make her happy."

"She was a promiscuous bitch."

Gideon hoped his father had no idea just how low his wife had sunk before her death. At the time of her suicide, she'd been pregnant with another man's child. He glared at his father. "That was uncalled for."

The viscount sat down behind his desk, his expression fierce. "So slashing her wrists and coming down dressed in her best white gown to display herself to your dinner guests didn't discompose you? I was there, dammit. I saw your face."

"Perhaps Caroline chose a rather melodramatic way to end her life but she was obviously distressed and not behaving quite as she ought." How in God's name had he ended up defending his wife? He should be in the diplomatic corps with Gervase negotiating with the French.

"Pah! She was as mad as a hatter." The viscount offered Gideon a brandy he was glad to accept. "Anyway, to get back to my original point. It is time for you to consider marrying again."

Gideon prayed for patience. "After enduring the first wife you chose for me, I am a little reluctant to allow you to interfere and choose my second."

"I don't care whom you choose, dear boy, as long as she is presentable. I just want you to marry. The succession must be secured." There was an almost fanatical glint in his father's eye as he thumped his desk, making the brandy slosh out of his glass.

"Gervase is married. Mary is married," Gideon said. "You will have more grandchildren than you need soon."

"Gervase chose to marry Eden Carstairs. She might well be barren. Your sister Mary's children will bear another man's name and inherit another man's title. You are my eldest son. Our lineage has remained intact, handed down from father to son for over two hundred years. I don't intend to break it."

It always came back to that. Gideon's grandfather was the Marquess of Valdemare, an ancient title Gideon stood to inherit after the death of his father, the current heir. Harcourt Hall was over four hundred years old and looked more like a medieval fortress than a stately home. Gideon loved every brick and stone of it. The estate was as much a part of him as his twin and just as embedded in his soul.

If Caroline hadn't chosen to end her life so dramatically, Gideon would've been happy to raise her child as his own. He'd told her as much but that had infuriated her even more. She hadn't wanted his sympathy and understanding. He stared morosely into his brandy glass. The weight of his heritage and the need for an heir was a burden and a curse when his sexual proclivities were far wider than was considered acceptable.

He glanced up to find his father watching him. The viscount was no fool. Rumors of Gideon's sexual tastes must have filtered through to him.

"What if I choose to remain single?"

"And allow someone else to inherit what should belong to your children?"

Gideon shrugged. "By the time it happens I'll be dead and so will you. Would I really care if Mary's children, the Babbington–Thomases, became masters of Harcourt Hall?"

The viscount got to his feet, his gray eyes full of disdain. "I dislike your flippant attitude, Gideon. And yes, I believe you would care far more deeply than you are letting on." He leaned across the desk and swiped the brandy glass from Gideon's hand. "I will bid you good day, sir."

Realizing it was his cue to leave, Gideon pushed back his chair.

"I will think on what you have said."

His father didn't bother to reply as he started to open his mail. Gideon let himself out of the house and headed for his club. At least there he might shake off the feeling that he was five again. It began to rain as he skirted the corner of the square and looked for a hackney cab. He wished Gervase was here, but his brother was on the other side of the English Channel engaged in diplomatic work or busy fucking his enchanting wife.

Gervase would probably laugh at him and tell him to do what he liked and damnation to their father. Gideon envied his twin who had married against their father's wishes and was deliriously happy. Gervase had no notion of the burden Gideon carried as the heir.

A cab clattered up and Gideon climbed in and directed the driver to White's. Perhaps it was simply a matter of waiting his father out. He grinned at the thought of his father stubbornly refusing to die before he was presented with an heir.

His smile died and he stared out of the mud-spattered window. In the narrow social world of the *ton*, love matches like that of his twin were uncommon. Most of the women he encountered were perfectly willing to indulge his sexual appetites and expect nothing in return. In truth, until he'd encountered Anthony Smith, he'd assumed that no woman would ever arouse him again. Her open curiosity and her naiveté in a jaded, corrupt society captivated him from the first.

What was that quaint French expression? Ah yes, *un coup de foudre*, the lightning bolt of love or possibly pure lust. He grimaced. Now he sounded like a third-rate actor from a Drury Lane farce. Still, the thought of marrying another of his father's choices had to be faced and preferably avoided. Since his wife's death, he'd deliberately allowed the more male part of his sexuality free rein. Could it be that his horror of becoming embroiled in another damaging liaison had tempered his desire to have anything approaching a relationship with a woman at all?

Gervase would call him a coward for being unwilling to take a risk and find out if his unnamed new companion was worth loving. Gideon sighed. What the hell was he doing, worrying about happy ever after when he didn't even know her name? She might regret her experiences at Madame's and he might never see her again. But perhaps her appearance was a sign that his father was right and it was time to move on.

In the meantime, he contemplated his visit to Madame Desiree's that night. Would Anthony decide to trust him? The prospect of sparring with his newfound companion made Gideon's anticipation rise along with his cock. Surely there was no harm in enjoying the moment. He glanced at his pocket watch as the cab drew to a halt. In little over twelve hours he would have his answer. To his astonishment, he could hardly wait.

Antonia's fingers shook so badly that she fumbled the arrangement of her cravat for the fifth time. She gazed at the crumpled linen in despair. No one would ever believe she was a gentleman of the *ton* if her cravat looked like a dishrag. There was no time to retrieve another from her cousin's room. He might get suspicious if she took more. Charles was the penny-pinching kind of man who noticed such things.

With all her concentration, she managed to knot the linen and quickly stabbed a gold pin through the arrangement before it fell apart again. She ruffled her short hair and put on her waistcoat and coat. That would have to do. On her last day at Jane's, Lord Harcourt had sent her an unsigned note containing the date and time for their meeting which she was to present to the footman at the door of Madame Desiree's. She hoped she wouldn't be late.

Holding her boots in her hand, Antonia crept down the servants' stairs and headed for the kitchen door. It had been far easier to escape without raising the house when she stayed at Jane's. Now she was back with her cousin Charles, his mother and three sisters. All of whom swore they were light sleepers.

Orange light spilled from the wood oven and fireplace as she tiptoed past but no one seemed to be up. With a sigh of relief, she unlocked the back door and bent to put on her boots. She stifled a scream when a familiar pair of feet stuffed into worn purple slippers appeared alongside hers.

"And where do you think you are going dressed like that, miss?"

Antonia gulped in air. "Gwen, I need to do something." She squeezed her maid's plump arm. "Please don't tell anyone you saw me, I promise I will be safe."

Gwen frowned. "It's dangerous out there, bach. It is not like the countryside. You should go back to bed."

"I can't." Antonia gazed into her maid's suspicious eyes. "I'll be fine. If I don't return in the morning, ask Lady Jane where I am."

She kissed Gwen's cheek. "Have I ever lied to you? I promise I will be safe."

Gwen pushed her away. "Go then, and if I lose my job for this night's work, I'll be expecting you to provide for me for ever more."

Antonia chuckled. "You know I would do that anyway. Good night."

She escaped up the basement stairs into the thick fog. Thank goodness it was her old nurse and current maid who had discovered her. She was the only servant loyal to her in the whole house. She was used to Antonia's wild schemes and usually tolerant of her need to escape.

Antonia made her way to the busy thoroughfare beyond the elegant square of townhouses. A shrill whistle brought a hackney cab to her side and she quickly gave the driver the directions.

The butler at Madame Desiree's kept her waiting in an elegant anteroom just off the main hallway. Antonia paced the carpet, her hands behind her back. The imposing room was decked out in white marble and reminded her of a tomb. There was no fire in the grate. What if Gideon Harcourt had been jesting? What if he regretted his odd offer and didn't intend to turn up?

When the clock chimed midnight after an anxious twenty-five-minute wait, Antonia was ready to flee. She picked up her cloak and marched back into the hall.

"Leaving so soon, Mr. Smith?"

She halted at the front door and turned to find Lord Harcourt halfway down the wide staircase. He wore a black coat, cream breeches and a dark embroidered waistcoat. His golden hair shone in the soft candlelight as he smiled at her.

Antonia bowed. "I thought I had mistaken the date, my lord."

"Ah, no, the fault is mine. I was unavoidably detained." He held out his hand. "Perhaps you would forgive me and join me upstairs?"

Antonia studied his outstretched hand. Should she leave? Had he deliberately kept her waiting to test her mettle? She wouldn't put it past him. Something reckless buried deep inside her rose to meet the challenge in his gaze.

"I would be honored, my lord."

To her surprise they climbed two flights of stairs and he led her up to a smaller version of the first floor. Doors still lined the corridors but instead of names they bore only numbers. Gideon stopped outside the tenth door.

"Madame Desiree keeps these rooms for her special clients who wish to avoid the public nature of the downstairs salon where one might be recognized. I thought you might appreciate some privacy. This will be our room whenever we require it."

Antonia walked in and found to her surprise that the chamber seemed fairly innocuous. True, there was a large bed on one side of it but the other side was set out like a lady's sitting room with comfortable chairs and an inviting fireplace.

Gideon chuckled, making her jump. She hadn't realized how close he'd come up behind her.

"Did you think I might take you to my dungeon where I torture innocent maidens until they scream for mercy?"

Antonia moved away until one of the chairs was between them. "It's not quite what I expected to find here. It reminds me of my mother's private suite at home."

Gideon sat in one of the chairs. "I didn't want you to feel threatened."

She sat opposite him, hands clasped in her lap. "But why would anyone who seeks out the sexual extremes of a place like Madame Desiree's want to be reminded of their own home?"

"You'd be surprised what people desire. Perhaps it is simply that this room represents sanctuary and security to those who have lost it."

Antonia stared into his serene blue eyes. After her mother's death, her father had refused to touch anything in her rooms. Antonia had lived with the knowledge of her mother's possessions decaying behind a locked door for most of her life. She shivered.

Gideon frowned. "Is this not to your liking? We can move to another room."

"It is fine, my lord." Antonia smiled at him until he relaxed back into his chair.

"Did you manage to escape unseen?"

She made a face. "It's not as easy to run wild in London as it is in the countryside. I had to get past my maid first. I fear she knows me too well."

"Will she keep her counsel?"

"Of course." She returned his frank gaze. "But if I should not return, she will raise the alarm with my cousin Lady Jane."

He raised an eyebrow. "How very wise of you, my dear. I'll have to rethink my plans for your abduction and sale into slavery."

For some reason, his outrageous words calmed her fears instead of banking them. "I left a letter with my cousin Jane as to my whereabouts but not exactly whom I was with."

He nodded. "That was clever. I shall not fear for my life at the hands of your family then if you should go missing."

Silence fell between them, broken only by the snap of the fire. Antonia took a deep breath.

"What exactly are you offering to do for me, my lord?"

"What exactly do you want?"

"I want to learn about London society from a man's point of view. It's unfair that I should be expected to marry before I have any idea about the world. I want to judge my prospective suitors in their natural habitat."

"Like an elephant in the jungles of India?"

She shrugged. "If you wish to use that analogy, then yes. I believe men behave very differently when there are no women around."

"So you wish me to take you with me and guide you through the pitfalls of modern life." Gideon got to his feet and headed for a tray of drinks beside the fireplace. He poured two brandies and brought them back. "And what will I get in return for this charitable action?"

Antonia stared at him as he passed her a brandy. "What do you want?"

His gaze traveled down the length of her legs and back up. "I want the opportunity to seduce you."

"And if I do not wish to be seduced? What if I wish to remain a virgin for my husband?" She prayed she looked sincere. She had no intention of telling him that she hoped to remain untouched even after marriage.

"There are many paths to pleasure, Anthony. If I promise not to take your maidenhead, will you give me permission to teach you other ways to please both yourself and your potential mate?"

Her heartbeat increased as he fixed his gaze on her, a question in his eyes. She imagined his hands on her, his mouth pressed to hers. A strange warmth flooded her belly and heat blossomed on her cheeks. She couldn't deny that his sensual invitation intrigued her. Was it possible that despite her fears she could learn to gain pleasure from her body and from a man's without fully consummating the relationship?

She struggled to conceal her interest. A whole new world of sensual opportunity had been offered to her by a man she had only just met. A man who fascinated her in more ways than she could count.

"Why would you agree to this?"

He sipped his brandy and regarded her over the rim of his glass. "Because I am bored and because the idea of deceiving half of London excites me. You excite me."

Despite her secluded upbringing, she knew she should be wary of his intentions. Her staid female relatives would be screaming at her to run from the heat and calculated lust in Gideon Harcourt's eyes. But she wanted to live dangerously. She wanted to know and understand what she feared.

She put down her untouched brandy and held out her hand. "I agree to your conditions."

Gideon folded her fingers back into her palm. "Don't be so hasty. There are several other matters we need to agree upon before we proceed."

She frowned. "Like what?"

"I don't even know your name."

She laughed to disguise her relief. "It's Antonia. But you may call me whichever name you please. What else?"

As she laughed, Gideon studied her mouth. Her lower lip was plump and sensual, her small teeth white and even. Her calm demeanor aroused him. He sensed that she met everything with open and honest bravado. How frustrating for her to be trapped in female form in a time when women were supposed to be frail and dainty and need protecting from any harsh breeze. He could picture her fighting alongside Queen Boudica, her spear dripping blood, her magnificent gray eyes blazing with righteousness.

"In private, I prefer Antonia," Gideon said. "I also suggest we meet here and use this establishment to convey messages to each other, do you agree?"

Relief lightened her countenance. He repressed a smile. The secret of her true identity was obviously something she intended to guard from him. She had no idea that he had already set one of his most trusted servants to the task of following her home tonight. To all intents and purposes, her secrecy simply added to his enjoyment and that was his primary reason for embarking on this masquerade, wasn't it? And the thought of bedding her...

He sat forward and held her gaze. "Before you agree to go any further there is something you must understand. The very fact that you sit before me makes me suspect you are both stubborn and headstrong. If you enter my world, you must agree to abide by my decisions. I will not tolerate disobedience."

She raised her chin, dissent plain in her gaze. "I am not allowed to question you?"

"Naturally, you may do so, but in the end, my decision is final. If you cannot agree to that, there is no point in pursuing our association."

She sighed heavily. "Am I to exchange the tyranny of petticoats for the tyranny of a man?"

He smiled. "Ah, but I do not seek to crush you. I simply wish to keep you safe."

She studied him, her wide eyes as bottomless as a becalmed sea.

"I will try."

"Is that the best you can offer me?"

"It is an honest answer, at least."

He raised his glass to her and got to his feet. "Then it will suffice. Come now and allow me to undress you."

Her hands clenched on the arms of the chair. "I beg your pardon?"

"I've been staring at that rag wrapped around your throat for long enough. It is time to teach you about the finer points of male attire."

Antonia laughed again, a low musical sound which brought an answering smile to his lips. She followed him over to the full-length mirror beside the bed. In preparation for this moment, Gideon had ensured that a supply of men's clothing occupied the cupboards and drawers.

He extracted a clean white shirt and a cravat and laid them on the bed next to the new coat he had ordered for her.

Without looking directly at her, Gideon asked, "Will you take off your coat and waistcoat?"

She complied and stood, hands fisted by her sides in front of him.

"I assume you have bound your breasts?"

"Yes, although in truth, they are scarcely worth the effort."

He mentally applauded her bravery and wit despite her obvious shyness. It was probably the first time in her life that she had undressed in front of a man who wasn't part of her family.

"Will you remove your shirt?"

With a stifled sound, she pulled the shirt from her breeches and drew it over her head. Gideon made no effort to hide his frank perusal as he slowly circled her. Her skin was pale like the finest porcelain, her ribs clearly defined, her back narrow. Strips of linen were wrapped around her breasts, flattening them completely.

His cock stirred as he contemplated the hint of a darker shadow where her nipples pressed against the fabric. Soon he would like to suckle her through the linen, make her hard and wanting. Make her come. He took a step toward her and touched the soft hollow where her collarbone met her shoulder. She swallowed, her throat muscles working.

"You are very beautiful."

"I am too thin for current fashions. Perhaps that is why I look better dressed as a man."

He chuckled as he allowed the tip of his finger to trace the linen binding her breasts. "You may be right. In this instance, less may be more." Under his fascinated gaze, her nipples tightened, leaving the pattern of her arousal on the cloth. He flicked a finger over one hard tip, heard her gasp.

"The binding appears to be sufficient. Let's start with the clean shirt, shall we?"

Had she noticed the tremendous swell of his cock in his breeches? He turned her to face the mirror and dropped the shirt over her head. When she emerged, her face was flushed. Gideon helped settle the voluminous shirt over her body, allowing his hands to brush her skin at every opportunity.

He picked up the cravat and draped it around her neck. He stood behind her, his gaze meeting hers in the mirror. "A man's cravat says a lot about how he views himself in the world."

She snorted. "It is but a twist of linen and a pin. How can it be so important?"

"Because its arrangement, and the care and thought which goes into it, are meant for other men to admire and aspire to." He slid his fingers down the long strip of linen, his knuckles shaping the slight swell of her breasts. She followed the movement of his hands in the mirror and shifted restlessly.

"I do not wish to look like a dandy or a fop."

"You wish to look like a girl dressed up in her brother's clothes?"

"No, of course not."

He held her gaze in the mirror. "Then let me show you."

He slowly folded the wide length of linen into a neat series of pleats which he gathered at her throat.

"How do you do that so efficiently?"

He smiled at her. "Practice, I suppose. Hand me the diamond pin to your right." He secured the snowy folds of the cravat and adjusted the high points of her shirt collar around them. "There you see? Much neater."

Antonia studied her reflection, turning her head from side to side. "Will you teach me how to do this for myself?"

He pulled out one of the bureau drawers and showed her the rows of folded cravats. "Be my guest. You may ruin as many as you like."

She carefully unpinned the cravat, her face a study of concentration as she considered the folds he had made. While she worked, Gideon ordered some food and more wine. Before meeting her in the lobby, he'd spent a strenuous hour in bed with his latest inamorata in an effort to drain off his lust and make him fit to deal with Antonia. Despite his efforts, he was semi-erect and eager. It was a strange, if unnerving sensation after his year of near abstinence, to experience such intense sexual tension.

Under his father's watchful gaze, he would have to make an effort to peruse the latest female offerings of the *ton* as if he truly wished to marry again. If Antonia was more experienced, he might have asked her to pretend to be his potential bride. But under her calm exterior, he sensed she was truly afraid. Forcing her to masquerade as his latest flirt might destroy her courageous attempt to move beyond her fear. Most women bored him. He hated the way they fluttered around him, their willingness to be weak, their need to be emotional about everything.

Of course, there were always exceptions. Madame Desiree was one and his sister-in-law Eden another. Neither of them balked at demanding what they wanted from a man and both of them enjoyed taking sex to its limits. He truly believed

Antonia was capable of being as passionate and inventive in bed as he was. In some ways it was a shame that he was set against marriage. The pleasure of teaching her to enjoy and explore her own sensuous nature was too good to ignore and too important to rush. He smiled. Perhaps she might even teach him something.

"Oh bother! I thought I had it then."

Antonia flung another crumpled cravat to the floor to join the others she had already ruined.

"If you wish to act like a man, perhaps you should strive to improve your choice of curse words."

She glanced up to find Gideon watching her, a slight smile on his lips. He leaned against the mantelpiece, displaying his long languid frame to advantage.

"Damnation, then." It was amazing how comfortable she felt with him, despite his outspoken desire to seduce her. She picked up another cravat and this time managed to fold it to her own satisfaction.

He sauntered across to her, his critical gaze on her latest effort.

"Well done, that is almost passable. Now you need to tuck your shirt into your breeches, but before you do that, let me add something else."

Antonia's breathing hitched as he approached. He placed his hands on her shoulders and turned her toward the mirror. His hand traveled down over her stomach and slid inside her unfastened breeches. He cupped her mound, his fingers warm and solid against the softness of her linen.

"I believe we had this discussion once before. Despite the fact that you have men's small clothes on, you do not have the required shape here to pass muster."

Antonia made herself breathe out, wondered if he could feel the gathering dampness between her legs. "Are you suggesting that men look at each other's..." She flapped a hand in the general direction of her groin.

"Of course they do. There is an instinctive urge to compare oneself with another male." He grasped her wrist and drew it behind her. "Measure me, feel how I fit against your hand."

He curved her palm under the compact, heavy weight of his balls. She shut her eyes as he redirected her to press against the solid column of his shaft. He shuddered slightly as if her touch pleased him. Growing bolder now, she moved her hand, gauged the width and length of his erection, felt it grow and stiffen beneath her questing fingers. A pulse began to throb between her legs, directly beneath his fingers.

"Surely, most men do not walk around in a state of arousal?"

He chuckled, the sound low, enticing her to entertain wicked thoughts. "Most men, no, thank God. That would be painful. Luckily, the cock we fashion for you will not be so easy to arouse."

Keeping her hand pressed firmly between their two bodies, he eased her breeches down to her knees. "A carefully folded stocking sewn into your small clothes should do the trick. Don't scream."

His fingers slid under the cloth and touched the soft curls of her mound, making her jump. He molded a thick stocking against her flesh, brushing the swell of her sex with every small adjustment. With each sensual tug, she found herself gripping his cock more tightly, inhaling the scent of her own arousal through her open breeches.

He flattened his hand over the stocking and pressed it against her before he slowly withdrew his fingers. She watched in the mirror as he did up the buttons on her breeches. To her surprise, they did fit better.

She flexed her hips, felt the rough caress of the wool. Gideon wrapped his arm low around her hips holding her close and crushed her fingers against his huge erection.

"When you get home, sew the stocking in place outside your small clothes. It will feel more comfortable without the wool being in close contact with your skin. You might prefer to use a silk stocking if you wish to be considered less well-endowed."

"It is fine." She licked her lips, saw him watch her, felt bold enough to do it again. "It feels as if someone is caressing me."

He cupped her mound, molding the stocking closer. She tilted her hips and hoped he'd ease the ache he had created. "Aye, like the rub of a man's finger over your clit or the underside of his shaft on your sex before he enters you. I like that. I like to imagine you becoming aroused, your pussy getting ready to welcome me."

His teeth settled on the curve of her earlobe and he bit down. She shuddered as his cock continued to rub against her fingers. Some of his words sounded crude and unfamiliar but even in the short time she had spent with him her body had begun to understand what he meant.

She struggled to remember what she was supposed to be doing.

"Do I look presentable, then?"

He studied her reflection. "You look like a woman who needs to be pleasured by a man."

"That was not our intent, was it?"

"It was always mine, but perhaps I have pushed you too far this evening."

He stepped back, his voice cool, and removed her hand from his cock. She wrapped her arms around herself at the sudden loss of contact. She felt like a lapdog whose owner no longer thought she was amusing.

"Then should I go now? Are you done with me tonight?" For the first time, she noticed there were no clocks in the room. It was if time stood still for their erotic interlude.

"Perhaps you should put your waistcoat and new coat on."

Antonia grabbed the waistcoat Gideon held out to her. If it hadn't been for the substantial swelling in his groin, she might imagine he had lost interest in her. He stood back and watched her struggle into her coat. She held her tongue, refusing to indulge in a fit of womanly pique that she suspected he would treat with indifference.

His gaze swept her figure and she drew herself up to her full height. It was a pleasure to stand next to a man who towered over her. She was tired of following her aunt's advice and bending her knees in an effort to look shorter.

"Walk across the room."

Determined not to balk at his commanding tone, Antonia obeyed. When she reached the far wall, she turned and walked back.

Gideon shook his head. "You need to take longer strides and carry your shoulders higher."

"If I carry my shoulders higher, my breasts stick out."

He considered her for a long moment. "They are bound, are they not? Therefore you should not have a problem, Try it again."

Antonia set her teeth and repeated the process, trying to model herself on her cousin Charles.

"That was better."

"Good, shall I go now?"

He raised an eyebrow. "Are you so eager to be off then, my dear? Have I failed to live up to your expectations? Did you imagine I would plunge you into my male world of debauchery without teaching you how to protect and disguise yourself?"

Antonia stared at him. What had she expected? Not this buildup of tension and awareness in her body which made her want...what exactly?

"You have been more than kind. I appreciate all you have done for me." Her words sounded false and stilted to her own ears. He must think her a fool.

Gideon took her hand and kissed her palm. "Next week, I promise you we will move on to other more interesting male pursuits. Now perhaps you should go home."

She was being dismissed like a child. Next he would pat her on the head and give her a penny like her father used to do. Why did everyone think she was so biddable? Greatly daring, she stood on tiptoe and kissed his mouth. His arms coiled around her waist and held her close but he didn't kiss her back. Trapped in his embrace, she simply glared at him.

"I am sending you away for your own good, you know," Gideon murmured.

She wiggled to get away but he easily held her still.

"Nonsense, you are sending me away because you are bored with me."

He laughed. "There are a lot of things you don't understand about men yet, my dear. One of them is that you can only tempt a man so far." He set her away from him. "If you were a man you would understand that after touching a woman so intimately, I'm hard and ready to fuck."

His blunt language, which she suspected was intended to shock her, simply reawakened the slumbering heat he'd aroused earlier. She reached out and stroked the bulge in his breeches. "Does it hurt you to be like this?"

He didn't pull away from her touch. "Not yet, but it will ache like the devil if I do not attend to the matter soon."

"You will manage this by yourself?"

He smoothed a hand over his groin, curving her fingers around his hard flesh. "I'll decide that when you have gone."

Her innate curiosity bubbled over. "How?"

"Dammit, Antonia, how old are you? Do you know nothing of what goes on between a man and a woman?"

"Twenty-six, but you have not answered my question."

He sighed. "What the hell was I thinking when I offered you my services?"

She ripped her hand out from under his. "I am not a child. You promised to be honest." She headed for the door. "If you will not be frank with me about a man's true desires then there is no point in continuing this charade. Good night, my lord."

"If you wish to stay and watch me pleasure myself, you may."

Antonia stopped, her hand flat on the door panel and took a deep breath. Did she? She paused as she heard the creak of Gideon settling into a chair, the soft brush of disturbed cloth, the faint scent and sound of the wet slickness of his desire. She slowly turned around.

His breeches were open, his left hand wrapped around the huge shaft of his cock. He used his right hand to slide down his foreskin to reveal the glistening purple tip. Antonia bit her lip as a drop of liquid slid down the side of his heated flesh and came to rest on his hand.

He turned from his contemplation of his shaft and looked up at her. "Have you ever seen an erect cock before?"

She trembled as a long-buried memory resurfaced to torment her. She'd been too bold and allowed her anger to lead her into a situation she had no ability to control. With a gasp she grabbed the handle, wrenched open the door and ran.

Chapter Three
ഌ

Antonia squinted at the ragged edge of the embroidered rose. She lacked concentration and her needlework, never her finest accomplishment, suffered. If her Aunt Flora saw the mess she'd made of the cushion cover she was supposed to be sewing, she would insist Antonia pull out the stitches and start again.

"Did you hear me, dear?"

She hastily covered her work and looked up to see her aunt staring at her.

"I said that we will be attending the Markhams' ball this evening. It is the first large ball of the season. Charles particularly wants you to make a good impression on the Markhams' eldest son, Douglas."

"I will do my best, Aunt." Antonia tried to smile back as her aunt frowned over her spectacles. Flora had been married to Antonia's deceased uncle and now kept house for her son.

"You do not seem very excited at the prospect of entering the *ton*, my dear."

Antonia sighed. "At my age, I feel rather too old to be prancing around like a debutante. I would much rather stay at home and read a good book."

"La, Antonia, how can you say that?" Her cousin Deborah looked amused. "I can't wait to be introduced to all those fascinating, eligible men."

"Deborah, that is exactly why your brother and I feel that you are far too young to be out," said Flora. "Your manners and opinions are too high-spirited for a young lady of good family."

"I was only funning, Mama. Antonia knows that."

Antonia winked at her fifteen-year-old cousin. They shared a love of open spaces and an impatience with London society that mystified the other members of the family. In an attempt to divert Flora's attention from Deb, Antonia spoke up.

"I promise to do my best to engage the interest of Mr. Douglas Markham, and to enjoy myself. Is that sufficient?"

Flora settled back into her chair and continued with her sewing. Antonia stared out of the window which faced the windswept square. Would Gideon Harcourt be among the guests invited to the Markhams' ball? Would she see him in his element? Surrounded by his peers, a particular lady hanging on his arm?

"Ouch!"

She rubbed her finger where she'd jabbed herself with the needle. She hadn't thought to ask Gideon if he was married. What if he had a wife? Was she taking him away from another woman? It was not as if she intended to become his mistress or anything. She just needed his expertise. Antonia dropped her needlework into her sewing basket and got to her feet.

Flora's head jerked up. "Where are you going, dear?"

Antonia held up her still bleeding finger. "I need to deal with this cut before I stain my work. I'll just go and find Gwen."

In the safety of her bedroom she rang for her maid and then sat down at her small desk. After nibbling on the end of her quill pen for a considerable time, she wrote. "Dear G., are you married? Yours, respectfully, A."

She frowned down at her words. Was she too abrupt? What else was there to say? After her panicked retreat from Madame Desiree's the previous week, she'd thought long and hard about returning. The sight of Gideon's cock had dredged up a half-forgotten childhood memory of her mother seeking sanctuary from her husband in Antonia's bed. She had claimed Antonia was sick and needed her.

When her drunken father stormed in, Antonia had tried to hide. She had ended up trapped against the wall while her father ripped open his breeches, held her mother facedown on the bed and had her anyway.

Her grip tightened on the quill pen and she forced the hateful images away. She had two more nights until she was due to meet Gideon again. If he had a wife, it gave her a perfect excuse to end matters between them. Surely he would understand.

Gwen appeared, carrying a roll of linen and a jar of ointment. Her thick gray hair was braided tightly around her head, her mouth permanently turned down at the corners.

"I heard you cut yourself, bach. Let me bind it for you."

Antonia held up her finger. "It was only a little prick; there is no need to..."

She allowed Gwen to fuss over her for a minute before returning to her desk. She wrote Madame Desiree's address and the room number on the note and sealed it with wax. "I need this delivered as soon as possible."

Gwen sniffed. "Have you become so high-and-mighty living in London that you've forgotten how to say please and thank you? Why not give it to the butler? He will see to it soon enough."

"I don't want anyone in the house to know, that's why I am asking you, please."

Gwen took the note and stuffed it in the pocket of her apron. Her Welsh accent always thickened when she scolded Antonia. "I hope you know what you are doing, child. I'm not going to explain to your family if you turn up missing."

"It's only a note. I'm not planning on eloping or anything." Antonia hoped she sounded more confident than she felt. Gwen was no fool. "I'm just asking for advice."

Gwen mumbled something under her breath as she opened Antonia's wardrobe and retrieved a pale pink dress. "Mrs. Callender says you are to wear this tonight."

"That dress drains all the color out of my skin," Antonia grumbled. "Why did Flora have to pick that one?"

"Perhaps she doesn't wish you to look your best. I think your dear aunt wants you to marry her brother, Thomas."

Antonia shuddered. "Thomas Quinn is twenty years older than me, he wears a corset and his false teeth clack like castanets when he laughs."

"Be that as it may, but he would surely enjoy your fortune."

Antonia stared at herself in the mirror. Of course, now she was an heiress, most men would probably find her attractive. Was being married for her money a worse fate than being married for her looks? She thought about the freedom Gideon offered her and how disappointed she would be if he turned out to be married. At some basic intimate level, he understood her need to explore that which frightened her. Was it possible that his instruction could help her to overcome her fears and have a normal marriage?

She leaned back as Gwen coaxed her short hair into curls and threaded a pink ribbon through them. Tonight would be but the first of many such balls, parties and receptions she would be required to attend. It was hard to remember her duty to her family when her heart dreaded the very thought of a marriage. Arranged marriages were the norm but they seldom resulted in love. Her parents had disliked each other on sight yet her father had wanted an heir and insisted on bedding a woman who didn't want him near her.

Her father's rages and her mother's shrieking defiance echoed in Antonia's mind. Her childhood was scarred with the pain of their battles and the pathetic graves of her many siblings. All in pursuit of a male heir. Her fingernails dug into her palms. She didn't want that. Only the thought of Gideon

Harcourt kept her from running back home to Wales—and her desperate plan to find a husband willing to leave her alone in return for the money she brought him. Men were fickle creatures. Her father's promises to her mother had meant nothing. Antonia took a deep steadying breath. If she wished to avoid a marriage that made her a slave to her husband's dynastic ambitions, she had to keep her wits about her and try and gain every possible advantage from Gideon. He was offering her the opportunity to observe the male of the species at close quarters. Surely that would be enough to stop her from making a terrible mistake?

Gideon spotted Antonia Maxwell in the crowded ballroom. Her height and her indifferent expression made her stand out amongst the crowds of overdressed young women and their chaperones. Not many women had the perfect bone structure to carry off the shorter more daring hairstyles but Antonia did. He concealed a smile as her gaze wandered around the room. Was she hoping to catch sight of him? He had no intention of advertising his presence. Better that she believed he was in ignorance of her place in society and the rumors that had already sprung up in the clubs as to her fortune.

He regarded her critically. The pale pink dress did nothing to enhance her subtle beauty. Her shoulders were narrow and her breasts small. The tapered satin skirt concealed the length of her legs and made her look too thin. Gideon frowned. She looked more comfortable in her breeches than in a gown. He knew Antonia had money, so why was she dressed like a poor relation?

Perhaps she was attempting to scare off her suitors. She had intimated as much to him at their last meeting. Betting in the clubs indicated that her cousin Charles, reluctant to lose her wealth, intended to marry her to one of his own family or close political cronies. No wonder the poor girl looked so harried.

139

Antonia's Bargain

He hesitated and turned for one last look. It was obvious that she didn't fit into the ordered world of the *ton*. He'd always had Gervase to share his adventures with and a family name that allowed them to be "different". What did Antonia have? A fortune and a family shattered by unsubstantiated rumors of infidelity, madness and worse. Perhaps that was why he felt such a deep kinship with her.

Gideon made his way back to the entrance of the ballroom. He'd seen enough to satisfy his curiosity and assure himself that she was a lady. After retrieving his hat and cloak, he left the sealed note with one of the servants and asked him to deliver it to Antonia. Her anxious question as to his marital status intrigued him. Was she considering him as a candidate for marriage or worried that she might be about to consort with an adulterer? Both scenarios amused him greatly. His short note assured her that he was a widower and that he was looking forward to their rendezvous. He hadn't signed it. She would know who he was.

Without a backward glance he left the luxurious townhouse and headed for his club. After an evening spent fending off the fortune hunters of the *ton*, he imagined Antonia would be very pleased to see him in two nights' time.

Chapter Four

ഇ

"You came back then."

Gideon's languid voice made Antonia jump as she carefully closed the door behind her.

"Of course I did."

"Strange, I thought I might have scared you away last time. Do you normally leave your companions at a run?"

She forced herself to look at him. "I admit I was a little intimidated. Like all young ladies of a certain class, I have been kept in lamentable ignorance. Your..." She waved her hand at his groin.

"My cock? Don't be missish, my dear. Call it what it is."

"Your cock, then. It was much more than I expected."

He sat in a chair by the fire, one elegant booted foot propped up on the hearth. His black waistcoat was embroidered with jet beads and silver thread which glinted in the firelight.

"Bigger?"

Antonia shrugged. "Just more."

He frowned as he ran his hand over the front of his breeches. "You looked terrified when you saw my cock. Are you sure you are a virgin?"

"Yes." She stiffened as he got to his feet and sauntered across to her. She should have realized very little escaped him.

"There are men who are not as careful in dealing with virgins as I will be. There are even men who take advantage of their own kin." He halted in front of her, his blue eyes serious, his expression remote. "If you have been violated, I would rather know so that we can deal with it together."

"I have not been touched, I assure you."

He studied her for a long while and slowly nodded. "Then we will continue with our agreement."

She let out her breath.

"You look more like a man today, my dear." He flicked his fingers over the front of her breeches. "You have filled out."

"I merely followed your instructions, sir." Relieved that he had changed the subject, she held her breath as he studied her cravat. "I hope I pass muster."

His lips parted in a smile. "Show me how a man walks."

She strolled away from him, mindful of his gaze on her shoulders and carriage.

"That is much better." She walked back until she stood in front of him. His long fingers caught a curl of her hair and pulled her close. "You make a very pretty boy." His lips brushed her cheek and she shivered. He moved away and resumed his seat by the fire.

"Come and join me. Tonight we will discuss how to drink and how to gamble like a man." A card table sat between the chairs, an unopened bottle of brandy beside it.

Antonia sat down. "I have never touched strong liquor, sir."

"Are you sure you aren't a Methodist?"

"No sir, I'm a woman. We are generally considered too weak and feeble to drink anything stronger than lemonade or ratafia."

Gideon opened the bottle. "If you wish to visit men's clubs, you need to drink like a man." He frowned at her. "There is no point in pulling a face. I'm not suggesting you become a drunkard just that you appear to tolerate strong drink."

He sloshed some brandy into the two glasses and gave her one. She sniffed it gingerly and held it away. "Why would anyone want to drink this? It smells like decaying plums."

Gideon drained his glass and set it back on the table. "Perhaps I can make the taste more palatable for you." He leaned across and set his hands on her shoulders, bringing her to her knees in front of him. "Taste my lips."

Carefully she licked the outline of his mouth; the heat of the brandy stung her tongue and made her own lips tingle. He opened his mouth, offering her more. Greatly daring, she slid her tongue inside, enjoying the texture of his mouth, the way his particular spicy scent mingled with the brandy.

He slid his hand into her hair and angled her head, molding her mouth to his as he stroked his tongue over hers. She allowed him to take control of the kiss, resting her hands on his outstretched thighs, feeling the hardness of his bunched muscles beneath the cloth.

When he drew back, she blinked. "Do you always kiss your male friends like that?"

He held her gaze, his expression serious. "If I desire them, yes."

Antonia waited for his smile but it didn't come. She scrambled back to sit on her seat. "Was there something else you wished to show me?"

He glanced down at his groin. "I believe we had this discussion last week. You arouse me, I am hard again. You can choose whether you wish to aid me with that problem or not."

"You were right. The brandy did taste better on your lips."

He smiled at her abrupt retreat. "I suggest that from now on you try and drink it yourself. Kissing me in the middle of a gaming hell to enliven the taste wouldn't be a wise idea."

She contemplated the brown liquid. "Perhaps I might just take a few sips and pretend to drink the rest."

"Aye, I've heard some cardsharps tip the contents of their glasses down the inside of their shirtsleeves in order to appear more drunk than their victims."

Antonia peered down the cuff of her shirt. "I could probably manage that. I can practice at home."

Gideon picked up a pack of cards from the table. "Good, then let us move onto the more interesting part of our evening. Gambling."

He expertly shuffled the deck of cards and laid them on the table in front of them. "Men will wager on anything. Who has the longest cock, whose grasshopper can jump the highest, who can ride to Brighton in less than an hour. If there is a question about the outcome of any event, a man can usually find another fool to bet on it."

"And they say women are the weaker sex."

Gideon raised an eyebrow. "I'll pretend I didn't hear that remark. Tonight I intend to teach you how to play piquet."

Antonia patted her pocket. "I have little money on me, sir. How do you expect me to gamble?"

He shrugged. "Most men play on credit. Tonight we will play for other things." He fingered the lapel of his exquisitely cut coat. "We will play for each other's clothing."

Gideon waited to see if she would balk at his suggestion but she relaxed back into her seat. He picked up the deck of cards and showed it to her. "The game is played with a thirty-six-card deck by removing all the numbers below six except the aces."

He reshuffled the cards. "Normally we would cut the cards to determine who would be the dealer, but in this case, as you are a complete beginner, you will have to be content with me."

The game was complex but he was pleased to see she picked it up quickly. After a couple of practice games, she gathered the deck and handed it to him.

"I am ready to play now, sir."

He smiled at her enthusiasm and allowed her to win the early stages, resulting in the loss of his coat, cravat and waistcoat. Her face flushed with pride as she carefully laid out a sequence of three cards.

Gideon pretended to sigh. "Alas, you are too good for me."

She frowned. "I think you are lying, sir."

He revealed a run of four hearts. "I believe you are right. Take off your coat."

"I suspect I shall lose more than my coat this evening."

He risked a glance at her over the top of his cards. "I can promise you that you won't lose your precious virginity."

He'd already calculated exactly how many tricks he could afford to lose and yet still have her naked by the end of the night. But first, one more loss for him. He played his cards accordingly. What would she make of his unclothed chest?

After he lost, he took his time removing his shirt and left his breeches unfastened. Antonia seemed unable to look away from the sight of his uncovered skin. For the first time, he was glad he'd made some effort to retain his physique since his wife's death. He casually flexed his biceps. How would her fingers feel against his flesh, her mouth on his nipple?

With a deliberate effort, he returned his thoughts to the cards, even more determined to see her naked in the least possible time.

Antonia tried to calculate the worth of her hand for the ternary phrase of the game. Despite her early successes, she seemed destined to lose. She slapped down her cards.

"Three jacks."

"Four queens. Take off your waistcoat and cravat."

With trembling fingers, Antonia complied. Now, only her shirt protected her from Gideon's gaze. How many tricks did she need to win in the final stage of the game to prevent herself from ending up naked? Gideon stretched and the candlelight burnished his muscular frame. She wanted to lean forward and taste his golden skin.

"Are you ready for the final stage, sir?"

He shook his head as he tallied the scores. "Unfortunately, you have lost again."

"I know that, can't we move on?"

He showed her the score sheet. "I claim a repique. I have thirty points in hand."

"That can't be right!" She grabbed the sheet from him and did the calculation in her head. "Damnation. You are not going to demand another forfeit, are you?"

"Of course I am. Take off your shirt."

She glared at him for one hopeless second before wrenching the shirt over her head. "Are you satisfied now?"

Suddenly it was hard to breathe. She reminded herself that he had seen her like this before. He reached out and ran his finger along the line of the linen binding her breasts. Her nipples became instantly erect.

"Not really. You haven't removed the linen binding your breasts."

"You will have to win that privilege." She picked up her remaining cards and studied them carefully, trying to ignore the heat of the fire on her bare skin and the weight of Gideon's stare. She laid out her next card. He placed one on top.

"My trick, I believe," Gideon said, his voice calm.

Antonia stared down at the card table. He was right, drat him. "May I remove my breeches instead?"

"No. I want to see your breasts."

With all her courage, she got to her feet and slowly removed the linen bindings. She closed her eyes as Gideon rose too and moved toward her. With a soft growl, he settled his mouth over her breast and drew it fully into his mouth.

Awash with unfamiliar sensations, Antonia could only grab his hair and drag him closer. Soon her nipple throbbed in time to her heartbeat and her ragged breaths. He used his fingers to rub her other breast to complete her torment before changing sides. The ache between her legs intensified and she slanted her mound against the curve of his hard thigh in an instinctive search for release.

Her hands skimmed his naked back, dropped below the line of his opened breeches and met the rounded muscles of his buttocks. He groaned deep in his throat and jerked his hips against hers. When he abruptly set her away from him, she found it almost impossible to stay upright.

"We haven't finished our game yet," Gideon said. "We have one last hand to play."

She sank down onto the floor at his feet, uncaring of her nakedness, aware that her nipples stood out stiff and proud from his suckling. She yearned to drag them across the golden hair on his chest to renew the rough sensations he roused in her. Blindly, she stared at her cards. She couldn't even remember how to play the game. What else did Gideon intend to do with her?

She lost again and closed her eyes, waiting for his next command.

"I will give you a choice."

His words made her shiver with a mixture of longing and fear.

"You can remove your breeches or help me with what is contained in mine."

"Surely, as a gentleman, you will not make me do either of these things."

He laughed, a hint of steel in the sound. "A gentleman always pays his debts and that is what you wish to be, is it not? I will not allow you to shirk yours."

She opened her eyes. If she failed to choose, he would probably refuse to help her with her charade. Which path was less hazardous? Exposing her lower body to him or exploring his? She wanted to touch him so badly.

"I will help you with your breeches."

He smiled down at her, one hand resting over the swell of his cock. "There is no need to sound so miserable. You might find you enjoy the experience."

Antonia knelt up and laid a hand on his knee. "I will do my best to satisfy you, sir."

His fingers closed under her chin and brought her head up. "My name is Gideon. In such an intimate moment, I think you should use it."

She swallowed as he absently toyed with her nipple, sending stabs of pure lust straight to her sex. He took her hand from his knee and placed it beneath the open panel of his breeches. She almost gasped at the heat of his flesh and the steady thrum of the pulse beating through his shaft. He closed his fingers over hers, guiding them around the base of his cock. Thick coarse hair brushed the backs of her knuckles as she gripped him tighter.

"Now, follow my movements." He shifted his fingers until they worked his shaft, leading hers into the rhythm he required. She forgot about the strangeness of her position and concentrated on the hard slick feel of his flesh beneath her fingers and the wetness that soon coated them. His hips rocked into the movement and his widespread thighs brushed her sides as he moved.

"You have it now, don't stop."

He removed his hand, leaving her to work his cock by herself. Enthralled, she inhaled the salty musk of his seed and slid her fingers farther up. She shaped the bulbous head of his crown and the thick vein which ran beneath the head. He groaned and brought his wet fingers to her breast, his mouth to her mouth, enclosing her in a tangle of ferocious desire and need.

She pulled his shirt and breeches away to reveal his erection so that she could study her fingers clasped around it. His stomach muscles contracted as she stared at him,

"Do you like my cock?"

She nodded, still absorbed in her contemplation of this most male of mysteries. "It is threatening and yet, so perfect."

"Threatening?"

She licked her lips and he tugged her nipple hard. "Because I know it has to fit inside me and I cannot imagine how that could happen without pain. It looks too big."

"It would fit. I would make sure of that." He slid his hand between her legs. "You are already wet for me. With a little more work, I could have you begging for my cock."

She pictured him leaning over her, his hips inching forward as his shaft disappeared between her legs. She squeezed her thighs together and trapped his hand as a wave of fear washed over her. Her father had always hurt her mother. Desperately seeking common sense, she reminded herself that it was good to find out about passion and lust before she contemplated marriage. At least now she knew which activities to avoid. She didn't want to marry a man and become a slave to her own desires or his.

Gideon grabbed her wrist.

"Finish tormenting me, Antonia. Let me come."

She stared at his stiff, glistening cock. She could not allow the fear to rule her. "Is it permissible for me to taste you?"

He chuckled. "Wherever did you get that notion?"

She leaned forward until her mouth hovered above him and blew a warm cloud of breath over his aroused flesh. He wasn't her father. His scent intoxicated her, made her want to risk becoming more intimate with him. "I don't know. It just seems the right thing to do."

"God help me. A natural sensualist. I can't decide if I am delighted or horrified. Taste away."

She carefully licked the tip of his cock where a pearl-colored liquid emerged from the purple slit. She licked again, tasting him slowly, enjoying the feel of him in her mouth. His shaft pulsed against her tongue, the throb of his desire as steady and demanding as the beat of her own. Not so threatening now when she realized that one lick of her tongue made him shudder and arch against her. Was there power for a woman in this? Could she master a man when she held him in her mouth or inside her body?

"Pleasure me with more than baby licks. Take all of it into your mouth."

He sounded amused as if he thought her too much of a coward to dare to do it. She opened her mouth and took the first three inches of his cock inside. Would he like it if she sucked on him as he did on her nipples? His groan told her that he did. She carried on sucking, taking more of him until she feared she might gag. His fingers slid into her hair and held her close.

After a while, he pulled her away and replaced her mouth with their entwined fingers. "Finish me like this." Working together, they increased their speed and brought him to a climax. Antonia watched enthralled as his come spurted out of his cock and coated her hand.

She laid her head on his thigh as he sat back and stared at his now flaccid cock. Antonia moved her fingers away and he offered her his monogrammed handkerchief to wipe her hand. Would a well-brought-up young lady not be fainting in shock and horror after seeing a man in the throes of sexual release? Her skin felt thin, as if all her blood flowed too hard and too fast to be contained within it. Her sex throbbed as if she had denied herself something.

Restlessly, she rubbed her breast against the smooth satin of Gideon's breeches. He touched her shoulder, made her look at him.

"If you permit, I will pleasure you too."

She swallowed as his fingers shaped her small breast. "But I lost the game."

His smile was intimate. "Then, as the winner I will be gracious and share my victory with you." He came down onto the floor beside her and reclaimed her mouth in a deep possessive kiss. She moaned as he caressed her nipples into hard demanding points and then sucked on them again. He undid her breeches and dragged them down her legs. His hand settled over her mound against the wet curls covering her sex. She shuddered as his middle finger pressed the swollen bud of her clitoris.

"You must have touched yourself like this before."

She gazed into his eyes as he continued to stroke her. "I have, but..." She bit her lip. He stopped.

"But?"

"Nothing happens. I sense something should but after a while the ache becomes unbearable and I have to stop."

"Ah, but that is just when you should continue." He kissed her cheek. "When it becomes unbearable you are close to climaxing. You have to learn to let go. Let me show you."

He pushed her down onto her back and knelt between her legs, widening her thighs, exposing her soaking-wet pussy to his gaze. He bent his head, licked her clitoris with the tip of his tongue. Antonia almost leapt off the floor. She grabbed his wide shoulders to push him away.

"That is not decent."

He raised his head to look at her. "No it's not, it's sex. Decency should be left outside the bedroom door. This is just for pleasure and your satisfaction. I will not hurt you." He lowered his head and licked her whole sex until she forgot how to speak and could only whimper and moan with delight.

Pressure built in her belly and she writhed against it. Gideon continued to suck and lick her, holding her close even when she fought for release. She wanted to weep and scream and scratch his face as he continued to torment her. She dug

151

her nails into his shoulders; he grunted his approval and worked her harder.

Her focus narrowed to the sensations between her legs and the man who created them. She no longer had the power to make him stop. In truth, if he tried to walk away from her now she would scream with rage. She couldn't stop her hips from pushing upward toward his mouth as she climbed higher. He placed one hand behind her buttocks, tipping her forward and slid one long finger in past her anus.

With a groan, he sucked her clitoris into his mouth and used his teeth to hold her there. It was enough to send her spiraling into climax. She screamed and bucked against him as he continued to lick and suck and bite until she felt as limp and spent as a dishcloth.

When she opened her eyes, he was braced over her, his face wet with her cream. "Am I still a virgin?"

He raised one eyebrow. "Of course you are. I didn't penetrate your sheath at all."

"But I felt you inside me...I thought."

He smiled and reached forward. He ran his finger over her swollen sex until he reached the tight bud of her anus. "I entered you here. Did you dislike it?"

"No, it was interesting."

He sat up and drew her to her knees. "Perhaps we should call this card game a draw."

Her whole body ached as if she had caught a fever. "I have certainly learned more than I bargained for, sir."

He kissed her lips. He tasted of her. "My name is Gideon."

She stared at his mouth, amazed that he had used it on her sex with such explosive results. Unable to deny her need, she kissed him back, felt his tongue flick against hers in a subtle, gentle caress. He tasted of brandy and of her, a mingling of scents she would never forget.

He spread his fingers through the back of her hair, turning her face into his shoulder. "Next week, if you are agreeable, we will venture forth into the *ton*."

It took her a moment to realize what he meant. She felt her cheeks heat with gratification. "Have I passed all your tests then, Gideon?"

He released her with a last soft kiss, stood and buttoned his breeches. "Let us say, rather, that you are ready to begin the real challenge. When we are out on the strut, you will have to prove you are capable of carrying off your disguise alone."

She smiled brilliantly at him as he helped her to her feet and began to rearrange her clothing. She had feared the season would be all but over before Gideon deemed her capable of going out in her disguise. It occurred to her that despite their short acquaintance, he already understood her better than any of her family. He was offering her an opportunity she had never thought to have. A chance to investigate the men who were beginning to circle her like vultures, and decide whether any of them would be worth the terrible risk of marrying.

Chapter Five

ဢ

Gideon straightened his cravat as he entered the ballroom and automatically looked for Antonia. It was becoming a habit of his to search her out so that he could avoid her. He smiled at the ridiculous thought. Since meeting her, his life had expanded from its dour grayness and he'd even begun to enjoy himself again. Strange that a woman had done that to him especially after his decision to avoid them at all costs since his wife's death.

His smile died as his father strolled up to him, immaculate in pale blue and silver.

"Good evening, sir. I don't often see you at these affairs."

The viscount nodded. "I came to see if you were obeying orders."

If Gideon had possessed hackles they would have risen. "If you mean, am I on the prowl for a wife, then yes, I'm here, aren't I?"

"You don't have to like the girl. She doesn't even need to be attractive." His father paused to nod at an acquaintance. "You just have to get an heir on her. Remember, all women look the same in the dark."

Gideon glared at his father. Was he deliberately trying to goad him into a fight in the middle of a ballroom? "Are you suggesting I should only make myself agreeable to the ugliest and most desperate women in the room?"

The viscount touched his shoulder and maneuvered him into a convenient corner. "That's not what I'm saying and you know it. Despite your dubious reputation, you are a handsome and well-connected man." He lowered his voice. "But I'm not blind, Gideon, and I have traveled the world. I can appreciate that your tastes might lie in other directions."

Gideon stared over his father's shoulder as Antonia came into view. She was smiling at her cousin, her face flushed with animation. He remembered the taste of her sex and the way she'd clung to him while taking her pleasure. Was his father suggesting he knew what Gideon wanted? Since Antonia's arrival, Gideon wasn't sure he knew himself anymore.

"I couldn't do that to any woman, Father. Treat her like a broodmare. The end result would be the same. She'd grow bored and seek her pleasures elsewhere. I refuse to live through that nightmare again."

The viscount slapped him on the back "Find a woman who understands you, then. Find a woman like Gervase did who loves you for what you are, not for what you can bring her."

Gideon managed a smile. "Does such a paragon exist?"

"Well, Gervase obviously thinks so." The viscount frowned. "On the other hand, you might be surprised at what a woman is prepared to put up with to get a wedding ring on her finger. Choose a girl who will be too grateful to be married to care where you spend your nights."

On that less than helpful note, the viscount bowed and retreated to the card room. Gideon let out a breath. It was unlike his father to share a confidence with him. Their relationship had always been combative. Was the viscount getting soft or was his obsessive desire to have a grandson changing his staunch autocratic views?

"A penny for your thoughts, Harcourt."

Gideon turned to find his old friend Peter Howard at his elbow. Peter was one of the very few men he trusted with all aspects of his life. He had been the first to help Gideon carry his wife upstairs after her very public suicide and had, to Gideon's knowledge, never gossiped about that night to anyone.

"My thoughts are scarcely worth a penny." Gideon grimaced. "Family can be hell sometimes."

"I wouldn't know about that. I'm an orphan." Peter said. "The only family I claim are the Sokorvskys."

Gideon studied his friend's angelic expression. It was always difficult to know what Peter was thinking. His past had enabled him to remove all traces of emotion from his face. Gideon knew that as children, Peter and Valentin Sokorvsky had shared a hellish ten years as Turkish slaves. Perhaps that experience was more than enough to teach a man to control his every thought. Peter's outward serenity always reminded Gideon of a painted Renaissance saint.

Few people knew that beneath Peter's calm exterior lay a complex and deeply loyal man. Gideon had seen him with the Sokorvskys at Madame Desiree's on more than one occasion and had reason to know that Peter's sexual appetite was as individual as his own. Peter continued to study him, his gaze steady, no apology for whatever conclusions he saw being drawn in Gideon's eyes.

"Is Gervase still away?"

"He is." Gideon half smiled. "I miss him like the devil."

"I can understand that. The Sokorvskys are in Russia at the moment. I find myself with nothing to do."

They stared at each other in perfect understanding. Antonia whirled past Gideon in the arms of her dance partner. He was so close he could have touched her. Her unique lavender scent lingered in his nostrils, making him instantly hard. Gideon touched Peter's arm.

"I am bored with the *ton*. Would you like to spend the rest of the evening with me at Madame Desiree's?"

Two hours later, Gideon had drunk most of a bottle of brandy and lounged in front of the fire. Peter lay beside him. They had both removed their coats, waistcoats and cravats.

"Is your father pressing you to marry again?"

Gideon toasted him with his glass. "Is it that obvious? He wants grandchildren and I am supposed to provide them for him within the year."

"After Caroline, I can understand why you are reluctant."

Gideon held his gaze. "It's not just Caroline. Most women simply don't arouse me. It's not their fault, it's just that I dislike the idea of being smothered in petticoats and perfume and womanly sulks. I dislike being held hostage to their moods and their mamas and their childish innocence."

"It's hardly their fault, Gideon. Women are not encouraged to use their brains, are they? They are told men prefer them to be mawkishly pretty and completely innocent."

"And that's exactly what most men seem to want."

"Not all men. Valentin encourages his wife to pursue both her musical career and her mathematical studies."

"Valentin is an exception and you know it." Gideon sighed as Peter smoothed his hand over his thigh. "I know I am being unfair. Most women are as chained to their destiny as I am." He bent his knee, allowed Peter to move his fingers farther inward. "The interesting thing is, I think I have found what I want."

Peter cupped Gideon's balls. "A man or a woman?"

Gideon reached across to slide his fingers beneath the open neck of Peter's shirt. He tugged gently on his nipple ring. "A woman who only chooses to acknowledge me when she is dressed as a man. Take off your shirt."

"I can't say I'm surprised. A woman masquerading as a man would suit you perfectly."

Gideon raised an eyebrow as Peter continued. "I know you've chosen to bed mostly men in the last few years, but I've never believed your heart was in it."

"You haven't?"

"Just because you've tried to convince yourself that you prefer men, doesn't mean that it is the truth."

"And how would you know this?"

Peter locked gazes with him as he removed his shirt to display his lean muscular chest and scarred skin. "Because I spent ten years of my life in a Turkish brothel and I've been in every sexual situation imaginable. You use men because you believe they can't hurt you like Caroline did. If you truly preferred men, you'd let them fuck you as well and you don't."

"Perhaps I'm one of those men who believe that if they don't allow themselves to be fucked, it means they aren't a sodomite."

"You're not like that."

Gideon let out his breath. How was it that Peter thought he could see things so much more clearly than he could? "Does that offend you?"

"Me?" Peter grinned. "No, because I have no preference either way. I'm happy to fuck or be fucked by either sex."

Peter was tanned darker than Gideon, a legacy of his years in captivity. He knelt between Gideon's outstretched legs, the crown of his long cock already showing through his unfastened breeches. He tugged at the fastenings of Gideon's breeches. Gideon stayed his hand.

"Wait. Why are you so certain that you are right?"

"Why are you even asking me that? It's very simple. Despite all your lovers, how many men have you fallen in love with?"

Gideon stared at him, his thoughts in turmoil. "None."

"How many women?"

He shrugged. "Only my wife and look what came of that."

"And now you are obsessed by another woman. I rest my case."

Peter removed his hand from Gideon's breeches and knelt up. "Are you worried that this woman truly prefers to be a man?"

"In the sense that she prefers her own sex? No. I think this is more of a way for her to explore her own sexuality and avoid the things that frighten her." Gideon frowned. If Peter was right, she sounded just like him. "But that is certainly something I should investigate."

Peter groaned as Gideon leaned forward, sucked hard on his nipple and slid one hand down the back of his breeches. "God, I've missed being touched." He shuddered as Gideon gently squeezed his balls. "If she trusts you, surely you can persuade her to want you as a woman wants a man?"

Gideon's cock swelled at Peter's obvious pleasure. "She wants me, but I have already promised her I will not take her virginity." He took Peter's hand, placed it over his covered cock and waited until he began to move his fingers. "Hoist by my own petard."

Peter grinned. "Your petard feels remarkably fine to me. Let me attend to you."

"Let's see who gets attended to first."

Gideon shoved Peter onto his back and straddled him. He pressed his satin-covered cock against Peter's half-uncovered erection and enjoyed the pressure and roughness of the rocking motion. Satin against skin, smoothness against hot, hard flesh. For him, touching a man could be so much simpler than touching a woman. There was no fear of being too rough or too demanding. No fear of becoming emotionally involved. A man simply used his own strength to control his lover. With a hoarse shout, Peter grabbed Gideon's arm and rolled him onto his front. Gideon's shirt ripped as it was pulled over his head.

Facedown on the carpet, he shuddered as Peter dripped warm oil on his naked back. He tried to roll over. Peter held his arm clamped to his side and brought his knee up and planted it on Gideon's back. Gideon grunted as his hips and swollen cock were ground into the carpet.

He tried to keep still as Peter spread the oil over his skin. His heart rate increased, mimicking the thick steady pulse of his thickening shaft until he groaned. Peter slid his hand around to massage Gideon's chest, grazing the hard points of his nipples.

"Don't you wish you'd taken off your breeches now, Gideon?" Peter increased the rocking motion of his knee. "Because I'm not going to help you out of them until you beg. And then I'm going to use my teeth."

When Peter shifted his weight to reach for more oil, Gideon half rolled to one side and dislodged Peter. With a growl he pinned him beneath him.

"That's better." He bent and nipped Pete's nipple. "I always prefer to be on top."

Peter slid his hands up over Gideon's taut stomach and massaged more of the sandalwood-scented oil onto his chest. "Does she let you touch her like this?"

"To some extent. I have made no secret of my desire to seduce her."

Peter's nimble fingers eased beneath the closed waistband of Gideon's breeches and down between his buttocks, pulling the front even tighter over his straining cock. Gideon gritted his teeth. All he could hear was the thunder of blood pumping through his constricted shaft. "She refuses to tell me her real name. She refuses to acknowledge me at the *ton* balls we both attend."

"You have approached her there?" Peter gasped as Gideon wrapped a fist around his cock. "From what I saw this evening, you were avoiding someone, not courting them."

Gideon worked Peter's cock, his strokes hard and fast just as he knew his friend liked it. "It's true; I haven't approached her yet in her proper milieu. I've been hoping she'd come to me."

"You're an arrogant bastard. I'll come for you if you keep that up."

Gideon grinned down at Peter and kept up the fast pace. "You need this more than I do." He bent his head to suck Peter's nipple, his left hand slid beneath Peter's balls and headed toward his arse. "Let's see how quickly I can make you beg."

Antonia curtseyed to the Scottish Lord Kinsale, her latest partner and allowed him to take her back to her aunt. He was one of her cousin's preferred suitors which meant he was dull, worthy and annoying. Despite being only thirty, his manners were those of an elderly gentleman. He treated Antonia like a child which did nothing to endear him to her.

At the start of the ball she believed she had glimpsed Gideon by the door talking to an older man who resembled him enough to be his father. Gideon's expression had not been pleasant. He disappeared soon afterwards in the company of a tall blond man and had not returned.

She fanned herself and sipped at the lemonade her partner provided her with. "Lord Kinsale, can you tell me who that distinguished gentleman dressed in silver and blue is?"

He frowned and raised his quizzing glass in the direction of her pointed fan. "That is Viscount Harcourt DeVere, the heir of the Marquess of Valdemare. Have you met him before?"

Antonia shook her head. "I thought I might have, but I was mistaken."

"He doesn't frequent *ton* balls very often. Rumor says he is trying to scare up a wife for his eldest son and heir, Lord Gideon Harcourt."

"Really?" Antonia pretended to flutter her eyelashes. "Does Lord Harcourt need help to find a suitable woman?"

Lord Kinsale patted her gloved hand. "Some might say he needs all the help he can get. His first wife died in mysterious circumstances and gossip has it that Lord Harcourt was the reason for her demise."

Antonia studied the tall figure across the ballroom. As if he felt the weight of her stare, he turned and bowed to her. "Did Lord Harcourt murder his own wife? How exciting!"

"Hardly, my dear. But most of the mothers here might be a little reluctant, despite his wealth and rank, to let their daughters marry a man with such a murky past."

Lord Kinsale seemed to enjoy telling the tale. Had Gideon caused his enmity or was it merely the jealousy of a plain dour man for a handsome popular one? Jane appeared at Antonia's side.

"Are you talking about the Harcourt family?" She winked at Antonia. "I heard the viscount was asking about you and your fortune, cousin. He seems determined his son should marry again." She glanced around the crowded ballroom and pouted. "And how naughty of Gideon Harcourt to disappear just as the dancing started."

"Perhaps it was a good thing he left," Antonia said.

Both Jane and Lord Kinsale stared at her.

"I know from my own limited experience that it isn't at all amusing to be watched and gossiped over by the *ton*. Poor Lord Harcourt has probably had to endure it more than once."

Where had he gone? She imagined him at Madame Desiree's, a beautiful woman naked in his arms as he made love to her. She wished she could just walk out like Gideon could without having to involve herself in a million excuses of poor health and petty lies.

With an airy laugh, Jane linked arms with Antonia and drew her away from Lord Kinsale toward the ladies' retiring room. "Are you mad?" she hissed. "Never praise one gentleman when you are standing next to another unless you are trying to make him jealous."

Antonia shut the door and draped her shawl over the nearest chair. "What are you talking about?"

"Your defense of Lord Harcourt. Have you even met the man?"

"No, I haven't, but that doesn't mean I can't sympathize with him."

Jane patted her fat curls. "Gideon Harcourt doesn't need your sympathy. He is a dangerous man. If he believed you were interested in him he would probably eat you for breakfast and spit you out before tea just to teach you a lesson."

"What has he done to gain your dislike?"

"I don't dislike him, Antonia. After all, he will be a viscount one day and a marquess after that. But some say he drove his wife to kill herself because she could not provide him with an heir."

A cold fist coiled in Antonia's stomach. Her father had done as much to her mother by insisting on endless pregnancies even when the doctors advised him it was dangerous to continue. Was Gideon capable of driving a woman to her grave? She pictured his face, the hint of command in his words as he insisted she must obey him.

"I still think it is unfair to gossip about a man who is not here to defend himself."

Jane pinched her cheek. "You are so naïve. Society thrives on the misfortunes and triumphs of its members. As soon as Lord Harcourt finds a wife and settles down with her, all this will be forgotten."

Antonia picked up her shawl and headed back to the ballroom. Would Gideon provide her with an explanation if she asked him for one? Did she even have the right to ask? Her association with him was only temporary. She had no cause to alarm herself as to his future plans for his wife.

One of the reasons she tried to avoid Gideon at social functions was her fear that once they met officially, she would be forced to reconsider her relationship with him. It suited her to have him on the fringes of her existence. He was her exciting secret, her tantalizing would-be seducer, the man who allowed her to be wild and passionate and daring. If she acknowledged him within the repressive boundaries of their class, would he change? Would he come to represent as big a threat as any other available man?

She sighed as her next partner, another of her cousin's choices, came toward her. Perhaps it was better to ignore the gossip and simply pretend to know nothing at all.

Chapter Six

⅏

From the outside, there was nothing to differentiate the four-story townhouse in one of the shabbier streets of Pall Mall from any of its neighbors. Soft rain blew into Antonia's face and she huddled deeper into her new cloak. At least her men's clothing offered better protection than the flimsy muslins she normally wore. Gideon had also provided her with new boots and a hat that actually fit her. She followed him as he mounted the steps and knocked on the scarred green door with his cane.

The door opened a crack and a thin stream of yellow light illuminated Gideon's face. After squinting at them for a long, unnerving minute, a huge black man dressed in faded blue and gold livery flung the door open wide. His fierce expression melted into a wide smile.

"Lord Harcourt. Welcome to Harpy's, it's good to see you again."

Gideon handed the man his hat and cloak. "It's a pleasure to see you too, Bill. Are you still boxing?"

Bill took Antonia's coat and hat and laid them over his massive arm. "No sir, I ain't. I'm getting too old for that lark and the wife won't stand for it anymore neither."

"I'll wager you are more afraid of your wife than you are of your opponents."

"That's the truth, sir." Bill grinned, displaying his four solitary teeth. "And with good reason." He gestured at Antonia. "Is he with you?" She held her breath as Gideon nodded. Bill bowed and pointed up the stairs. "Then have a good evening, sirs, and good luck."

Antonia edged past the huge man and followed Gideon up a narrow flight of stairs. The smell of tobacco and cheap spirits that wafted down the hallway almost choked her. Her heart was already beating too fast. Would any of the other men see through her disguise or had Gideon taught her enough to make her invisible?

He paused at the door of the main salon and looked back at her, clearly offering her the opportunity to escape. She raised her chin and met his inquiring gaze without flinching. Deep inside her, beneath the fear, a bubble of pure excitement surfaced at her own daring.

The salon was crowded and dark. Several men clustered around a roulette wheel while others lounged in chairs set out around small tables and played cards. At least half of those present were in uniform. The rest seemed an odd assortment ranging from the overdressed fop to the average country squire. Antonia inhaled a thick haze of smoke underlaid with the scent of old sweat and desperation. A man stumbled into her, his expression dazed, his hands fumbling at his breeches.

"'Scuse me, young sir," he belched in her face, "I need a piss."

Antonia stepped out of his way as he lurched toward the chamber pots on the sideboards. No one else appeared interested in her. Most of the faces bore the same intent expression as they watched the turn of the wheel or the play of a card. Antonia tried to relax as Gideon handed her a chipped glass containing a brownish liquid.

"What do you fancy trying your hand at, young Anthony?" Gideon asked as she forced a little of the cheap liquor between her lips.

"Whatever suits you, sir."

He smiled and pointed out two empty seats at a nearby table. "Then let's sit here."

An older man with a thick red mustache dressed in the green uniform of a rifleman grunted as they took their places. "Harcourt. Haven't seen you in a while. Thought you'd given up gambling."

Gideon fished in his pocket for his purse and tipped a few coins and gold sovereigns into his hand. "Good evening, Captain Foster. Does a man ever stop gambling?" He handed Antonia half the coins. "Did you fear I had reformed?"

Captain Foster gathered the cards and shuffled them. "Dead or rolled up more like."

"I fear to disappoint you, but I have plenty of funds at my disposal."

"Good. I need a new uniform."

Antonia frowned at the captain dealt everyone two cards. What on earth were they playing and how dare Gideon drop her into a situation like this?

He murmured in her ear. "This is *vingt-et-un*. It's not difficult, you'll pick it up in no time, just follow my lead."

Twenty-one? Gideon picked up his cards and studied them. Antonia did the same and then tossed a sovereign onto the pile. She had two kings. What did that mean?

She watched as the other four players either held onto their hands or asked for another card. By the time Gideon laid down his cards to show the queen of hearts and an ace she thought she had the general idea. She shook her head when the dealer offered her a card and waited until he revealed his own hand which didn't match Gideon's but totaled the same as hers.

The pile of money in front of Gideon grew steadily as the game progressed. After a short while, Antonia had no coins left and simply watched. Gideon sat at his ease. One long-fingered hand holding his cards, the other relaxed around his glass. Unlike his opponents, his expression gave nothing away. While he played, she took the opportunity to scan the room for any of her potential suitors. She thought she caught a glimpse of one of her cousin's friends at the roulette table but she couldn't be sure.

Kate Pearce

Finally Gideon gathered his money and stood up. Antonia was quick to follow him. He bowed to the other men. "Gentleman, it's been a pleasure."

Captain Foster snorted. "I see you've not lost your touch, Harcourt. Won't you stay awhile and allow me to win some back?"

"Unfortunately, we must leave. I promised my young relative here a tour of the delights of the city, and this is but our first stop."

Captain Foster winked at Antonia. "You lucky dog. I wish I'd had a relative like Harcourt to show me the town. You'll be fortunate to get home before dawn and I expect you'll sample plenty of prime skirt along the way as well."

Gideon maneuvered Antonia toward the door and down the stairs. Inside his coach he dumped the pile of coins, bank notes and scrawled IOUs on the seat between them.

"Count this, would you?"

Antonia sorted out the pile and calculated the total. She stared at Gideon. "You won over a hundred pounds and we were only there for half an hour."

He raised an eyebrow. "Is that all? Of course we must also include your losses."

She straightened in her seat. "You gave me twenty guineas. I will pay you back out of my quarterly allowance."

His heavy lidded gaze swept over her. "I would prefer to receive my payment now. Come and sit on my lap."

He arranged her over his thighs so that she straddled him. "Did you enjoy your first glimpse into my world?"

She hesitated as he unbuttoned her waistcoat and pulled her shirt from her breeches. "It was not as exciting as I thought it would be. Most of the men there did not seem to be enjoying themselves much."

"You sound disappointed. I took you there first to show you how the average man about town gambles." His fingers

168

settled over her bound breasts. "Gambling is a serious business. Fortunes are lost and gained in an evening's play. The amount of money I won this evening might mean the difference between a man's survival or his complete ruin."

She closed her eyes as her nipples tightened between his finger and thumb. His erection settled against her mound, rocking into her with the movement of the carriage. She sighed as the now familiar heat of her excitement began to grow. Gideon was like a drug. The more he touched her, the more she wanted him. Would any other man be able to make her feel like this? Somehow she doubted it.

"What are you thinking?" He kissed her ear, his cheek smooth against her skin, his sandalwood scent as beguiling as the finest champagne.

"I believe you are leading me astray."

He chuckled and settled his hand over her buttocks, pressing her closer. "And isn't that exactly what you wanted?"

She stared into his amused eyes. "I'm not sure. I didn't realize I would enjoy being seduced so much. It makes me forget why I started this masquerade in the first place." His teeth grazed her lower lip and a pang of pure lust shot straight to her sex. "I didn't know that being touched so intimately could be so pleasurable." She licked the now tender spot on her lip. "My mother seemed to find only pain in her couplings with my father and none of the excitement I feel."

"Perhaps your father was an inadequate lover."

"Perhaps you are an exceptional one."

He smiled at that and spread his fingers over her buttocks, lifting her into the swell of his cock. "I'm not one to boast but..." He kissed her hard, his tongue plunging into her mouth until she squirmed against him. He winced and grabbed her hips.

"Be gentle with me, my cock is tender."

Antonia remembered how early he had left the ball on the previous evening. Her chest tightened with a sensation she refused to acknowledge as jealousy.

"Is that why you left the ball? To slake your lust?"

He caught her chin in his fingers. "Do you want me to answer that?"

A spark of bravado shot through her defenses. "Why not? You offered me your expertise."

"I'm sore because my lover sucked and bit my cock too much. Although I can assure you I didn't complain at the time." His expression darkened. "Now it's my turn to ask you a question. How did you know I was at a *ton* ball?"

She licked her lips as he continued to stare at her. Was he asking her to reveal her identity to him and if so, what effect would that have on their relationship?

"I was there with my family. I saw you leave."

He studied her as if waiting for her to say more. She continued to look back at him.

"You can't hide from me forever, Antonia." Gideon picked her up and dumped her on the seat beside him, scattering the pile of money all over the carriage floor. It hurt to breathe as she struggled to douse the rise of her arousal. Her breasts ached to be touched and an insistent throb between her legs begged to be satisfied.

Gideon bent to kiss her, his mouth hard and demanding. When he finally raised his head, he was breathing as harshly as she was. Perhaps he was not as unaffected by her as he tried to pretend. The reckless streak within her demanded she find out how far she could push him. She forced herself to sit still and not press shamelessly against him. He gestured to her untucked shirt.

"We will arrive at our second destination at any minute. Make sure you are presentable."

Gideon swept past the butler at White's and headed for the porter's desk. Antonia's refusal to tell him her full name had obviously rankled. She knew it was inevitable that they would meet in the narrow social world they both inhabited, but she wanted to prolong the moment for as long as possible. She waited as he signed her in the visitors' book.

"This is my club. We will pay a visit to the first-floor gaming rooms."

She scanned the elegant vestibule as an elderly gentleman staggered out of the dining room. The smell of overcooked beef and stale cabbage followed his unsteady progress as closely as a dog at his heels. The place looked duller than Harpy's.

Gideon led her up the stairs, pausing to bow to his acquaintances and to murmur the hope that his father wouldn't turn up and complicate matters. She caught her breath and bumped into him when he stopped abruptly at one of the massive sets of doors.

"You will probably see a few more faces you recognize in here, so I suggest you try and remain as inconspicuous as possible. Women are not allowed in White's."

He smiled, and she sensed that his amusement at bringing her into such a male bastion of power had temporarily canceled his frustration. He opened the door and bowed. "Welcome to Hell."

At first glance, the rooms appeared even quieter than the one at Harpy's even if the setting was more opulent. Gleaming oak-paneled walls were covered with portraits of past monarchs, club members and racehorses. The men remained the same, their intense interest fixed on the play, oblivious to her arrival. Gideon touched her arm.

"This time we will play piquet."

He led her to an empty table and called over a waiter. He exchanged a few coins for a brand-new pack of cards and set about sorting them. Antonia took the opportunity to take a furtive glance around the room. At a table by the roaring fire, she noticed two of her cousin's favorite candidates for her hand, engaged in a game of cards. Neither man looked happy as they contemplated their cards. She stiffened as she caught her name.

"Are you having any luck with the Maxwell chit, Kinsale?"

"If I am, I'm unlikely to tell you."

Douglas Markham snorted. "She's not exactly a beauty, is she?"

"Who cares when she has all that money? If I marry her I'll keep her stomach full of brats and let her live in the country out of my sight."

Antonia found her fingernails digging into her palms. She was being discussed with a coarseness she found offensive. They might at least pretend to be interested in her for herself. But then why should they? In the company of other men there was no reason to flatter her.

Gideon cleared his throat. "Are you ready to play, Anthony? And didn't your mother ever tell you not to eavesdrop?"

She managed a tight smile as she picked up her cards. "You will have to lend me some money, sir. I still have no coin."

He handed her fifty gold sovereigns. "If you lose these, I will expect you to obey me without question for the rest of the evening."

"I thought I had to do that anyway."

He raised an eyebrow. "But you don't obey me. Tonight you will."

She swallowed slowly. Too aware of the tightness of her nipples where his fingers had been so recently, of the pulsing ache of her sex where she yearned for his touch. "I will have to play very carefully then."

Within two hours, her last sovereign was gone and Gideon had moved on to another victim. Antonia stood and watched the play of the cards until she felt confident enough to saunter around the room. It was difficult not to display her amazement at the sums of money that changed hands at the tables. Gideon's earlier winnings were as nothing here. As the evening progressed, IOUs piled up, promising payments of unimaginable size.

Antonia began to detect which players were truly confident and which were on edge. She also took note of which of her suitors were in desperate financial straits. Despite the lavish apartments, the games played here were far more deadly and serious than those at Harpy's. Although the same air of heightened desperation and tension was present, the high stakes made matters more deadly.

A young man stood up and almost knocked her over as he pulled back his chair. He bowed jerkily to the man at the head of the table.

"If it pleases you, Lord Delamere, I will settle with you on the morrow."

"But it does not please me." The man sifted through the crumpled notes in front of him. "By my reckoning, you owe me at least ten thousand pounds."

"Are you suggesting I do not intend to honor my debts?"

The men around the table fell silent, all eyes fixed on the older man.

"Of course not, Lord Hartford."

Antonia edged farther back into the shadows against the wall. Lord Delamere's contempt and deliberate hint of doubt in his question were meant to be obvious to everyone.

"I will send my man of business to see you tomorrow morning, Hartford. Perhaps you will find it easier to deal with him."

She resisted an urge to hold Lord Hartford back as his hands fisted. To her relief, he simply bowed. "I look forward to it."

She let out her breath as he headed for the door. The vacant, stunned look on his face left her in little doubt that he had no idea how he intended to pay such a vast sum of money.

Lord Delamere chuckled as the door shut quietly behind Hartford. "He is a foolish pup. Perhaps it is time for him to learn not to try and ape his betters." He motioned at one of the younger men sitting to his left. "He's a friend of yours, isn't he? May I suggest you follow him and don't allow him to do anything foolish like blow out his brains? I'd hate for my man to have to deal with that mess in the morning."

The boredom in his voice made Antonia long to slap his hard, cynical face. She almost jumped when Gideon touched her shoulder.

"Are you ready to leave?"

She was more than ready. It seemed that beneath the veneer of sophistication all men cared about was money. How on earth did she expect to find a way around that?

Antonia was quiet when she reached Gideon's carriage. He studied the serene lines of her face, tried to remember when he had ever thought her plain. One more stop was planned for the evening. His cock throbbed and hardened at the thought of her reaction to his last choice of entertainment. He touched her cheek.

"Is something wrong?"

She looked away from him. "It's just occurred to me that men always win in the end."

"Not according to some of the women I know."

She studied him, her expression serious. "I thought I could avoid my destiny by learning to understand men and using those discoveries against them."

He took her hand in his and stroked her fingers. "There is nothing wrong with your reasoning. In truth, women have been managing men like that for centuries."

"By using their bodies or their wealth to secure themselves the best alliance?"

Her flash of temper aroused him. "And what is wrong with that?"

Her chest rose and fell in agitation. "Because it shouldn't have to be like that."

He slid his arm around her back and pulled her close. "Why not? Because you are too afraid of your own sexuality to try it? Wouldn't you like to rule me? Wouldn't you like to see me on my knees begging you to fuck me?" He kissed her hard and possessively. With a moan she kissed him back, her fingers tight in his hair.

He dragged his mouth away from hers and stared into her passion-filled eyes. "You promised to obey me this evening."

"Only if I lost all your money."

"You did."

She met his gaze head on. "Then I suppose I will have to."

The carriage stopped and Gideon reached across to open the door. "Good, because I have a surprise for you."

Antonia gulped as Gideon led her into the ground-floor parlor of the house in Hans Town. It was furnished in shades of red and gold like a shabby theatrical version of a sultan's harem. A number of women in various stages of undress sprawled amongst the low couches and cushions. A few men already occupied some of them. One man had his hand down the front of a bored-looking woman's corset as he enthusiastically pumped himself against her thigh like a dog in heat.

"Ah, Gideon."

A large elderly lady dressed in a flowing violet bed gown advanced and kissed Gideon on both cheeks. "We have not seen you here for a long while." She gestured at the women who were all staring avidly at him. Antonia noticed that the lady's French accent was as false as the color of her hair. "Is there anything in particular you require?"

Antonia cringed as Gideon slapped her hard on the back. "Actually, Madame, I've brought one of my cousins here." He winked suggestively at the room at large. "He's never been to town before. I promised to show him a good time."

Her cheek flushed so red she could feel the heat. She glared at Gideon but he refused to acknowledge her.

"I thought perhaps Louise might teach him a few tricks to take back home to Wales with him."

A tall red-haired woman rose from one of the cushions and walked across to Antonia. She studied her for a minute before nodding.

"I would be delighted. Go up to my room at the top of the stairs. I will join you in a moment."

Face still flaming, Antonia allowed Gideon to lead her away. "Do you expect me to watch while you have sex with her?" she hissed.

"Not at all, I'll be doing the watching."

She stared at him openmouthed. "As soon as she undresses me she'll know I'm not a man."

He shrugged. "So?" He opened the door and pushed her inside. The small room smelled of stale perfume and sex and was dominated by a large four-poster bed and a floor-to-ceiling gilt mirror.

"Gideon…"

He caught her chin in his hard fingers. "You promised to obey me this evening. If you refuse to keep your promises then why should I keep mine?"

She remembered her desire to see how far she could push him and licked her lips. "What if I wanted you to break them?"

He brought his head down and kissed her, the slow sensual attack left her trembling and wide-eyed. He drew back a scant half inch, his voice a mere whisper of sound. "I want you to enjoy this. I want to see you come while I watch. Is that too much to ask?"

She could only shake her head at the sexual promise in his words. So much for dominating him. All he had to do was kiss her and she wanted to agree with everything he said.

Before Antonia could form a reply, Louise appeared through a connecting door in the wall. She wore an open green silk dressing gown, a black corset and stockings. Her eyes widened as she took in their closeness. Gideon stepped away and bowed.

"My cousin is a little shy. I promised to stay with him and offer my...expertise."

Louise gave a soft laugh. "You mean that I should treat him just as you tell me to."

Gideon placed a substantial stack of gold coins on the corner of Louise's dressing table. Antonia studied Louise's face. She guessed the woman was about her own age, although the lines around her mouth suggested life had not been as easy for her as it had been for Antonia.

"I've always appreciated your intelligence, Louise, and your discretion." Gideon pointed at the red satin counterpane which covered the four-poster bed. "When you have finished undressing him, I'd like to see you both kneeling on the bed." He drew up a chair, placed it at the foot of the bed and sat down.

Antonia's anger fled and was replaced by anticipation. Was she really so desperate for Gideon's approval that she would allow another woman to touch her? Dammit, it seemed that she was. Every time he asked something of her, he pushed closer to the wildness that slumbered within her. She had also begun to understand that if she chose to let it free, he would be there to fan the flames and catch her as she burned.

Louise giggled when she finally pulled off Antonia's shirt. "It seems as if your cousin is confused. Does she really believe she is a man?" She flicked one of Antonia's erect nipples, making her shiver.

"Perhaps that is why I brought her to you, Louise. I thought you could help clear up any confusion."

Refusing to reply to Gideon's pointed remarks, Antonia was soon stripped naked by Louise's knowledgeable hands and led to the bed.

Gideon sat and watched as Louise climbed up behind her. He tossed two leather ties onto the counterpane. "As my cousin is so innocent, perhaps you might restrain her. God knows what she might do in her passion."

Antonia bit down on her lip as Louise bound her wrists to the two end bedposts. Her promise to obey Gideon had led her into deep waters. Her traitorous body still hummed with the anticipation of pleasure and release. She knelt up on the bed, naked and aroused and felt no shame.

"Fondle her breasts, Louise. Tell me how she feels."

Antonia shivered at Louise's touch. The lace bodice Louise wore beneath her silk bed gown scratched Antonia's back, adding to the prickling sensations already crawling over her skin. She looked down as Louise's fingers closed gently over her nipples, coaxing them tighter and tighter. Louise rolled them gently between her finger and thumb. Antonia found she was unable to look away.

"She is beautiful, sir. She cannot hide how much she wants you."

"Show me her sex. Is she wet for me?"

Antonia held Gideon's gaze as Louise parted her flesh and stroked the swollen wetness within her pussy.

"Oui, sir, she is soaking. Shall I slide my fingers inside her and show you how quickly she will come for you?"

A moan escaped Antonia's lips as Gideon shook his head. "No, for she is a virgin. But we will make sure she comes in other ways. Oil her for me, would you?"

Antonia inhaled a heady mix of spice and orange in the warm oil as Louise slowly spread it over her breasts. God, after Gideon's priming in the coach, she was so close to coming. Did they know that? Did they like to see her writhing on the edge?

Louise slid her fingers over Antonia's sex and plucked at her clit, rubbing it until Antonia tried to move her hips into the rhythm but her bonds held her close.

"Take off the rest of your clothes, Louise and then go back and kneel behind her."

Louise finished undressing and climbed back onto the bed behind Antonia. Gideon moved his chair even closer. When he sat down again, his face was a bare inch from Antonia's pussy. His warm breath tantalized her swollen flesh. She wanted his mouth.

"Gideon."

He looked up at her, his expression inquiring. "What?"

She realized he was not going to make it easy for her. "Please touch me."

"Where?"

Louise returned her attention to Antonia's nipples, her now oiled fingers making them gleam like two hard red berries. Her own generous breasts pressed hard into Antonia's back.

"Touch my sex, oh God, please, touch me there."

"Louise, show me where she means."

Antonia groaned as Louise's clever fingers exposed her swollen clit between her finger and thumb. Gideon leaned forward and sucked it into his mouth. Antonia climaxed instantly, pressing herself into the welcome hardness and relief of Gideon's mouth as if her life depended on it.

He released her with a last long lick and sat back. "Whose touch do you prefer, mine or Louise's?"

His quiet question brought her senses to the alert. "Do you think I prefer women? Do you imagine that is why I'm doing all this?"

He smiled and slowly licked her cream from his lips. "It did occur to me."

"I have never lusted after my own sex."

Louise kissed her neck. "I'm sure I could change your mind, cherie, if we had time, and you weren't already involved with this particular man." She slid her hand around Antonia's neck and kissed her openmouthed. Antonia found herself responding as cream flooded her channel. Gideon licked it up with an approving murmur.

When Louise drew back, Antonia was panting and straining at the leather ties. Gideon smiled at Louise.

"Would you like to taste her, cherie? She is very responsive."

Gideon allowed Louise to kneel between his legs. With one hand he toyed with her breast. The other he placed between Antonia's thighs. He spread her labia with his long fingers, displaying her to Louise.

Antonia stiffened as Louise delicately licked her clit. Another climax threatened as Gideon added his fingers to the torment of Louise's mouth. Antonia came hard in long, pulsing waves, unable to stifle her screams. She vaguely heard Gideon's next instruction.

"Get back on the bed behind Antonia, and I will satisfy you both."

He slid his palm between Antonia's legs and kept going. The underside of his wrist pressed hard against her sex as he slid his fingers deep inside Louise. Antonia closed her eyes as he began to move his hand, listened to Louise's soft moans and enjoyed the friction he provided. Louise rocked her body into Antonia's, her mound rubbing against Antonia's buttocks.

Gideon thrust his fingers deeper. He fondled Antonia's breasts and drew her into a deep kiss as he worked them both. From under her lowered lashes she could see his covered cock rubbing against the silk counterpane. Caught up in a sensual web too exquisite to ignore, she and Louise came together with identical screams.

After her heart slowed down to a less frantic rate, Louise untied her. She pressed a kiss onto Antonia's lips. "Thank you for sharing Gideon with me. He is an exceptional lover." She winked at them both. "And if you should decide you do prefer your own sex, after all, come and see me again."

Antonia collapsed facedown onto the bed and lay there. The mattress creaked as Gideon joined her. She almost purred when he placed his hand in the small of her back. Lying like this, her slender figure displayed in all its glory made Gideon want to plunge his cock inside her until he ran out of come. He glanced at the clock. It was almost three. He had less than an hour before he needed to see Antonia safely home.

She didn't move as he carefully removed his coat and waistcoat. He took two pillows from the top of the bed and wedged them under her stomach, raising her buttocks. Without speaking, he retrieved the bottle of oil Louise had left on the nightstand. With practiced ease, he began to massage oil onto her skin, concentrating on the delicate swell of her buttocks and the soft skin between them.

"Oh, Gideon, that feels so nice."

"Yes, cherie, and if you relax, it will soon feel even nicer."

She stirred as he increased his strokes, opening her legs at his gentle pressure until the whole of her sex lay exposed to him. He leaned over her, slid one hand beneath her breast to play with her nipple and set his teeth gently at the nape of her neck. With his other hand, he carefully penetrated the bud of her anus, using the slick oil to ease his way, adding fingers until she easily took them all.

He bit harder as she began to move against his thrusting fingers. With a muffled cry, she dragged his other hand down to her sex and pressed it to her. With all the care he could manage he slid two fingers in her sheath until they met the barrier of her maidenhood. He increased the long, slow glide of his fingers until he felt her grip him and convulse in a tight-fisted orgasm. He came too and felt the hot pump of his seed soak into the satin of his breeches. Damnation, he hadn't been this aroused since he was at school.

His nostrils flared as he inhaled the potent mixture of their scents. Antonia represented everything he ever wanted in a lover and had never expected to find in a woman. Her courage, the sensual wildness within her that responded to the devil in him made sexual boundaries disappear.

Peter was right. Antonia wasn't the only one who needed to learn about love. He'd never felt this urgent need to surround and protect a man. In the last few years of his marriage, he'd simply used one part of his sexuality to suppress his desire for this. The scent of a woman, the sense of completion, the true urge to mate with a female that he'd denied himself for so long. He removed one hand from her pussy and stroked Antonia's hair with fingers that shook. Was he capable of breaking through the self-defeating barriers which held his emotions in place? Would she even want him too?

For a long while, he continued to hold her, his fingers still firmly embedded inside her. The urge to replace them with his cock was too strong to allow him to move away. He kissed her throat as an unwilling laugh shook through him. In a few short meetings she had changed his life. Bloody Hell. He was about to make his father a very happy man.

Chapter Seven

හ

"I'm warning you, Antonia. If you haven't decided which man you prefer, I will."

Charles stood behind his desk, his face flushed red as she continued to glare at him. At ten in the morning his study smelled of stale brandy and burnt toast. The thick brown curtains let in little of the gray morning light.

"You can't force me to choose a husband. I have my own money now and I'm not a child."

He sat back down. "Actually, I can. Did you even bother to read the exact words of our grandmother's will?"

"How could I when you refused to show it to me?" Antonia took a step closer to the desk, her gaze fixed on the pile of parchment beneath Charles' hand.

"Grandmother knew you were wild. In her will she stipulates that you only inherit if you marry well and at your family's direction."

Antonia rested her fingertips on the desk as panic threatened to overwhelm her. "I don't believe you. The money is mine. Why didn't anyone mention this before?"

Charles turned the page toward her and pointed at a paragraph halfway down. Antonia leaned forward to read the cramped script, her heart raced as if she were running for her life.

"No one mentioned it because it probably never occurred to anyone that you would think yourself capable of handling the money yourself. You are far too impetuous, my dear, to deal with such a responsibility. Obviously, you need a man to take care of such things for you."

He smiled indulgently and folded his hands flat on the document. "Let me make it even clearer for you. In order to gain control of your inheritance, you have to marry, and I have to approve your choice."

Antonia stared at him as her stomach threatened to revolt. How very like her grandmother to offer her freedom and then snatch it back.

"If I marry, the money becomes my husband's, doesn't it? I will find another lawyer. I will contest this."

"And shame your family? Haven't you had enough scandal in your life?"

Antonia swallowed hard, caught between a sudden desire to slap his face or run back to Wales. She couldn't face the humiliation and disgrace again, she just couldn't. Charles came around the desk and took her by the shoulders.

"If you can't decide on a husband by the end of the month, I will offer your hand to Douglas Markham. He is a good decent man who will treat you with the respect you deserve."

* * * * *

Antonia gathered the skirts of her pale blue gown and headed back to the ballroom. She failed to hide a yawn as Lord Kinsale bowed to her and moved swiftly past him even as he spluttered in indignation. After her late night with Gideon, she found it hard to stay awake and maintain her interest in yet another boring party. She remembered the press of Gideon's fingers deep inside her, the slight bruise on her throat where his teeth had grazed her skin.

How had she come to care for him so quickly? It wasn't just that he allowed her to experience physical pleasure, although that was incredible. It was that he made her feel safe enough in his arms to try anything, to fight her demons and win. The gossip about him, despite his family name, placed him firmly on the fringes of the *ton*. Not that he seemed to care. But, as an outsider herself, she thought she understood him better than most. It was obvious to her that his charm and handsome features concealed a loneliness that matched her own.

Earlier that day, when Charles called her into his study and asked if she'd decided on a husband yet, she found herself wishing for Gideon. If he wasn't already married, she suspected Charles would be considering marrying her himself. He'd droned on about respecting her family and doing the right thing until she'd wanted to scream. Her family hadn't cared to intervene when she'd been left in the care of a distant father and an old harridan of a grandmother. Only her inheritance had changed that and now even that was in jeopardy.

She paused at the entrance to the ballroom. Would it be possible for her to refuse to marry and give up the inheritance? She shuddered at the thought of being trapped at the mercy of her family for a home and an allowance. If she had no money she would end up as an unpaid servant or married off to one of Charles' lesser friends in return for some political favor.

Her desire to see Gideon increased. Surely he would help her forget the impending snare of marriage? Or would he find it amusing? Part of her wanted to spill out the whole embarrassing story and ask for his help. She stared at the glittering ballroom without seeing it. Her life seemed to be measured in each shallow breath she managed to drag into her lungs.

"Miss Maxwell?"

She glanced up as someone blocked her path. It took her a moment to realize that the gentleman addressing her was none other than Gideon's father.

"We sat next to each other at that dreary musicale this afternoon at the Oakham's. I'm Harcourt DeVere."

Antonia sank into a curtsey. "I remember you, my lord; you made a dull event very memorable." The viscount had made loud and disparaging remarks about all the amateur performers. He'd reduced one poor young lady to tears, before being persuaded to retire to the card room. She now knew where Gideon had acquired his cutting wit.

"I hope you will forgive an old man, but I would like to introduce you to my son. He's in need of a wife and I hear you are looking for a husband."

Antonia stifled a hysterical urge to laugh. Did everyone in the *ton* know that she was expected to marry? The viscount obviously favored a blunt turn of speech, which would have been refreshing had it not been about Gideon.

"It's very sweet of you to think of me, but I'm sure your son is quite capable of choosing his own wife."

She thought the viscount snorted under his breath but he tucked her hand into the curve of his arm and marched her back into the ballroom. Before she quite realized what he meant to do, she found herself confronting the broad back of her would-be seducer.

"Gideon, I've brought a young lady to meet you."

He turned at the sound of his father's voice. The irritation in his eyes faded as he studied Antonia.

"Sir?"

"This is Miss Antonia Maxwell. She tells me she is on the lookout for a husband."

"Surely she's a bit young for you?"

Antonia pretended to titter and tapped her fan on the viscount's arm. "Actually, I told your father that you were probably quite capable of finding your own bride."

Gideon swept a bow and gave her a devastating smile. He was dressed in flawless black and white and a single diamond glinted in the folds of his cravat. "There's nothing wrong in receiving a little help now and then, is there?" He took her gloved hand. As if on cue, the orchestra struck up a waltz. "Would you like to dance with me, Miss Maxwell?"

She bit her lip as she noticed Douglas Markham striding toward her. His proprietary expression was enough to send her into Gideon's arms. "I would be delighted, sir."

His hand slid around her waist, he grasped her fingers lightly and drew her into the dance. It was easy to relax into his arms as they slowly circled the ballroom.

"I apologize for my father."

She glanced up at him. "At least he is direct."

He grimaced. "That is true. Although I find it quite humiliating to be put on show like this."

"Then you should understand how I feel. Courted for what I have and not for whom I am."

He held her gaze, his blue eyes serious. "I know who you are."

She tried to laugh. "But you are not courting me, are you?"

Her question hung in the small space between them as they continued to dance to the music. All at once, Antonia found it even harder to breathe. A blur of bright colors swirled around her and the hum of conversation rose and fell like the subdued roar of an incoming tide. Exactly how would it feel to be courted openly by Gideon? Was she so frightened by her cousin's ultimatum that it now sounded like an excellent idea?

"You think I don't know how it feels to be courted for what I am?" Gideon said. "My father assures me that despite my reputation, any woman would be grateful to exchange vows to gain my rank and status even if I admit I will never care for them."

"Not all women are so desperate."

He smiled down at her. "Then you see, we have the same dilemma, neither of us wants what society dictates. Neither of us wants to be married for our money."

She avoided his gaze, uncomfortable with the direction of his thoughts. He gathered her closer into his arms, his thigh brushing hers with each step.

"Apparently even the gossip that I killed my first wife isn't enough to deter all of them."

Bitterness laced his words and his grip on her waist tightened.

"Did you kill her?"

He grimaced. "Who is being direct now? If you mean did I physically slice her wrists open then of course I didn't. Do I feel some responsibility for her death? Then, yes, I do. I failed her. I failed to understand that she was serious when she threatened to take her own life."

The music seemed to grow louder, the steady beat echoing in Antonia's ears.

"My mother killed herself," she whispered. "For a long while, I thought it was my fault because she hadn't wanted to get up and come and play with me at the lake. If I hadn't taken her there, perhaps she wouldn't have thought to simply walk in and let herself drown."

She wished she had a hand free to clap over her mouth. Why on earth had she revealed something so personal in the midst of a dance floor and to Gideon of all people? She truly had no defenses against him. Her feet faltered and she almost tripped. He deftly guided her out of the dance and toward a secluded corner.

He turned until his broad back concealed her from the ballroom. She shivered as he stroked a tear from her cheek with the tip of his gloved finger.

"Perhaps we share more than we think. Guilt is a hard master, isn't it?"

She drew in a deep breath and managed a smile. "The dance is over. Will you take me back to my aunt?"

He kept hold of her hand, his expression for once devoid of all humor. "Antonia, what's wrong?"

She fought back her tears as he continued to study her. If he didn't stop being so kind she would throw herself at his chest and be damned to the consequences.

"It's nothing, my lord. Perhaps I'm a little overtired."

He smiled at her, his lazy grin laced with sensual appreciation. "I'm not surprised. You probably didn't get much sleep."

It was difficult to tear her gaze away but she managed it.

"Will you take me back to my aunt, sir?"

"If that is truly what you wish." He was still watching her closely as he placed her hand on his arm. She tried not to dig her fingernails into his flesh. Couldn't he tell that she was frightened and cornered and desperate?

It was almost worth waltzing with Gideon just to see the mixed emotions on Flora's face when they approached. Horror mingled with pride as she stared at Gideon's imposing form. He bowed and released Antonia's hand.

"Thank you for the dance, Miss Maxwell. It was a pleasure." He bowed again at Flora, nodded to Charles and walked away.

"Well!" Flora said as she pinched Antonia's bare arm. "How did that come about? He is not the kind of man a young woman of your character should be encouraging."

"We only danced, Aunt. I was introduced to Lord Harcourt's father at the Oakhams. He introduced me to his son who apparently needs a wife."

Charles stepped between them. "Don't be too hard on her. Harcourt and his family have a great deal of political influence." His gaze became speculative as he watched Gideon prepare to leave the ballroom. "As Antonia said, there's nothing wrong with a dance now and then. I'm sure we can rely on her good sense not to allow any further liberties."

Antonia struggled with an insane desire to laugh. If only Charles knew the liberties Gideon took with her, he would be appalled. She hid her expression behind her fan.

"Of course, Charles. I will do whatever you think is best."

She watched as Gideon paused to speak to his father and then left the ballroom. The evening suddenly seemed endless, the company even more boring than usual. She glanced at the clock. It was almost midnight. Surely she had done her duty by now?

As they headed for the refreshment room, one of the footmen slid a note into her gloved hand. With a frisson of excitement, she slipped it into her reticule. With her aunt's gaze on her, she would have to wait until she reached the sanctuary of her bedchamber before she could read it. She reluctantly returned her attention to Flora who was complaining about an ill-fitting dancing slipper and waited impatiently for the hours to pass.

* * * * *

By the time Antonia reached Madame Desiree's it was two in the morning. Arriving home after one, she'd scarcely had time to read the note and change into her men's garb before she needed to leave again. Gideon's note had indicated she should just come up to their particular room. Why had he asked to see her? Was something amiss? The footman on duty simply nodded at her as she headed for the stairs. Her heart thumped uneasily against her ribs as she paused outside the door. Was this yet another test? How would she feel if she failed him? With all her courage, she opened the door and slipped inside.

She inhaled the sharp scent of sex and sandalwood as her gaze fastened on the ornate bed. A blond man, who she thought she should recognize, and an older woman lay entangled on the black silk bedcovers with Gideon. He looked up as she closed the door.

"Ah, Anthony. Please sit down."

She sat obediently in the chair Gideon indicated and he turned back to his two companions. Her heart rate quickened as the woman patted his bare shoulder. She'd never seen Gideon fully naked before. He was magnificent, his chest and stomach well muscled, his legs long and elegant. To her surprise, unlike the two men, the woman was clothed. She searched her emotions for a sense of shock at finding Gideon with another man and found instead intense sexual curiosity.

She returned her attention to the blond man who lay sprawled facedown on the sheets. Gideon tugged on the man's hair and made him sit up.

"This is my friend, Peter. I believe you met briefly at the Oakhams' party."

Antonia nodded, hoping her face didn't betray her confusion. He smiled at her as Gideon toyed with his pierced nipple.

"I suspect you are the reason why Gideon has been so demanding lately." He grimaced as Gideon pinched his nipple. "I didn't say I minded, did I?"

Gideon knelt behind Peter and wrapped his arms around his waist. "You are always very accommodating."

Antonia crossed her legs as Gideon slid his hand down to encircle Peter's half-erect cock. The woman crawled across the bed and got off. She winked at Antonia. "Don't mind me. I love to watch and I also can provide an alibi if the authorities want to know what two men could possibly want to do in a bed together."

She disappeared into the dressing room, leaving the door wide open. "Now that there are three of you, I'm going to finish the scarf I'm knitting. Call if you need me, dearies."

Antonia couldn't take her eyes away from the swift motion of Gideon's pumping fingers as he brought Peter fully erect. One of his big hands moved up over the hard planes of Peter's belly and settled on his left nipple. The two men moved together like a well-matched horse and rider, a combination of mastered strength and restrained power.

"Fuck me, Gideon, please. I need…" Peter's voice trailed off as Gideon urged him forward onto his hands and knees. His arm muscles flexed and quivered as Gideon drove inside him.

Antonia's sex pulsed with heat and warmth as she imagined the feel of Gideon's cock. She'd only had him in her mouth. Peter seemed to be in ecstasy. Without thinking, she slid her hand between her legs and pressed hard.

"Yes, touch yourself, Anthony." She jumped when she realized Gideon was watching her. "Share our pleasure."

With a moan, she undid her breeches and plunged her fingers into the slick wetness within. As Gideon resumed his powerful thrusts, she worked her fingers to the same rhythm, wishing they were longer and thicker and more like a cock. She could only get part of the way in before she met the barrier of her maidenhood and she needed more.

"Come here, let me help you." Peter's soft voice intruded on her sexual daze. She stumbled to her feet and approached the bed. "Take off your breeches."

She kicked her way out of the confines of her breeches and boots and scrambled onto the bed.

"Peter. She's a virgin. Don't press her too hard." Gideon remained braced over the other man, his cock buried deep inside, one hand still grasping Peter's shaft.

"Put your hands on my shoulders, *Anthony*, and kneel up," Peter said. She faced him and knelt within his arms. He grasped her ankles to anchor himself against Gideon's thrusts.

She shuddered as Peter licked the tip of her swollen clit and then sucked it into his mouth. She widened her legs, inviting him to delve deeper, desperate to feel his touch. He obliged, his tongue sweeping her aroused flesh in hard, demanding strokes. He shifted more of his weight onto his arms as Gideon worked him harder and faster.

She felt the now familiar growth of her climax as Peter mastered her with his tongue. She whimpered for his fingers in her sheath and then added her own.

"Gideon, I've got to come." Peter tore his mouth away from Antonia's sex, his hips angling sharply forward, now, his breathing uneven.

"You'll wait until I give you leave."

Antonia stared into Gideon's face, noted his taut control, the passion that threatened to erupt at any moment. She leaned closer and bit his lower lip hard. He groaned deep in his throat, his thrusts became shorter, his grip of Peter's cock tightened until his knuckles shone white. Her climax slammed through her and Gideon came too. Peter's come spurted between Gideon's fingers onto Antonia's waistcoat.

She relaxed her grip on Peter's shoulders and sat back on her heels as Gideon disengaged himself. Peter sat up, turned to Gideon and kissed his cheek.

"Thank you, my friend. With Valentin and Sara away, I thought I should go mad. Thank you for sharing yourself with me."

With a soft smile for Antonia, Peter strolled into the adjoining dressing room and began to chat with the woman. Gideon sat back, still breathing hard and made no effort to cover his nakedness or clean the evidence of his passion from his flesh. Antonia studied his sweat-slicked skin and the solid curves of his muscled arms.

"Do you let Peter do that to you?"

"Fuck me? No, I prefer to be in charge. Surely you have realized that by now?"

His studied air of unconcern struck her as unreal. Was he waiting for her to pass judgment on him? Had he hoped to shock her by inviting her to witness such an erotic display of male lust?

"Does it give you pleasure?"

He shrugged, the motion displayed his wide shoulders to advantage. "What do you think?"

Antonia let out a long breath. "My father…" He still watched her, his expression unreadable. "My father preferred his valet to my mother. I walked in on him once. His valet was doing exactly what you were doing to Peter. My father looked ecstatic." She pleated the silk cover in her fingers. "I didn't really understand what I saw. He told me that if I ever spoke of it he would send me away and never let me come home again."

Gideon nodded as though she made perfect sense.

"That is probably why your mother was so unhappy then. You should not feel guilty about her choice to end her life. She obviously thought she had reason."

His easy acceptance of her shameful secret made her want to cry. A glow of warmth eased the clench of long-held pain around her heart. "When did you realize you were this way?"

He smiled and leaned back against the pillows, some of his wariness disappearing. "When I was at school. Gervase and I were fags for one of the older boys who liked to fornicate with his juniors. Gervase hated it. I found that it excited me, the roughness, the possibility of pain, the sensation of physically dominating another male. As identical twins it was easy for me to pretend to be both of us."

"Did your wife know?"

He sighed. "Such a simple question, such a complicated answer. Yes, she knew. At first she enjoyed the fact that I encouraged her to try different sexual scenarios. Eventually, I realized her tastes for such games went far deeper than I was prepared to go and I chose not to participate."

"Did you make love to her like that?"

Gideon went still. "I don't understand."

Antonia gestured at the rumpled silk bed sheets. "The way you did with Peter. Can you do that with a woman?"

He drew his right knee up and rested his hands on it. "I've penetrated you there with my fingers. You must know you could take my cock if you wished to."

She held his gaze. "And if I wished to? I'd still be a virgin?"

"In the eyes of the church, yes. But some would consider you...compromised."

She stripped off her coat. "I am already compromised. I want to feel you inside me, Gideon."

A desperate sense of rightness enveloped her. It made perfect sense. Gossip had obviously lied about his part in his wife's death. He'd told her of his remorse. If Gideon preferred men, perhaps he would be amenable to her marriage bargain. Her wealth and complete discretion, in return for sexual freedom for them both. She had to prove her worth to him, now, before she lost her nerve.

He reached for her hand. "Antonia, you do not have to do this. I wanted you to see who I am. I wanted you to understand that I like to fuck—" She cut him off with a kiss. He groaned and kissed her back, crushing her to his chest. His hands moved under her shirt to touch her skin.

"Are you sure this is what you want?"

In a hurry now, she removed her waistcoat and cravat. Gideon sighed as she leaned in to kiss his mouth. His fingers fisted in her shirt.

"Keep this on. Unbind your breasts, but leave your shirt. In my dreams this is how you look when I take you for the first time."

Her sex swelled and throbbed at the dark possessive tone of his voice. "You have always wanted to do this to me?"

"From the first time I saw you staring into the fire in the salon downstairs." He hesitated. "At that moment, I didn't care whether you were a man or a woman. You just intrigued me and I wanted you."

He slid his hands under the shirt and gripped her hips. "I will make sure there is no pain. I will make sure you are ready for me."

Antonia licked her lips. His cock was already hard and ready to penetrate her. She was ready too. Part of her wanted it to be over. The rest wanted him to linger over every glorious second. To her disappointment, he climbed off the bed and went into the dressing room. She heard the sound of him washing and his muted farewells to Peter and the other woman.

When all was quiet, he returned. In his hands he held a box, which he laid on the bed. "These are things to ease my passage and make it more pleasurable for you."

Antonia opened the intricately carved wooden box. Inside was a crystal bottle of oil which she knew from her previous experiences would feel delightful against her skin. She picked up a flared glass ornament which was about the thickness of a whip handle and as long as her hand. She looked up to find Gideon watching her.

He took one of the ribbed pieces of glass and held it next to his cock as if comparing the size before choosing a larger one. "We can take our time over this. There is no reason to rush."

Antonia scowled at him. Who knew how long her burst of courage might last. "I want you tonight, Gideon. I think I've waited too long already."

He opened the bottle of oil and trickled some onto his fingers. She inhaled the scent of orange blossom and spices. "Then I will do my best to end that wait. Kneel up and put your hands at the top of the headboard."

She grasped the oak edging as instructed, felt the long tails of her linen shirt graze the back of her bare thighs. Gideon sat behind her and rubbed oil into the soles of her feet and up to her ankles. The only sound in the room was her harried breathing and the soft slick of the oil. His hands slid up to her knees, spreading them wider.

"You are tense. Try and relax."

He sounded calm, his movements unhurried as he concentrated on oiling her skin. "I have imagined doing this to you for a long while. I've also wanted you to do it to me."

"Rub you with oil?"

He chuckled, his breath warm on her skin. "Yes and have you suck my cock while you are about it."

A gush of liquid flooded her sex as she thought about his words. His fingers grazed the insides of her thighs. She wondered if he could feel the thick cream of her pleasure trickling down.

He drew in a breath. "Ah, you are wet. Let me see."

She shivered as he carefully folded her shirt up and revealed her naked buttocks. He nudged her knees wide. The subtle lick of his tongue between her thighs made her arch her back, giving him better access to her sex. He brought his oiled fingers up as well, toying with her clitoris as he gently probed her anal bud. Three fingers inside her now, her clit slippery with her own juices and the oil. She came with a soft whimper, hardly felt him replace his fingers with the glass rod until it was wedged deep inside her.

His hands moved to her breasts and cupped them. She let out a wary breath.

"The glass, it cannot get lost in there, can it?"

He took her hand and brought it around to her buttocks. "No, feel, these things are designed to stop that happening."

Her fingers closed around the flared base of the glass. It was much too wide to fit inside her. Gideon took her hand and returned it to the headboard. He knelt behind her, his large body pressed against hers from knee to nape. His cock, a thick hot presence against the small of her back. He returned to her breasts, his oiled fingers working her nipples into stiff aching points. She rocked her hips back against him and felt the glass rod within her move and stretch her flesh.

She shuddered as he used one long finger to stroke her clitoris. She struggled with the desire to come again. "May I touch you, Gideon?"

He removed his hands from her body and sat back on his knees, his fingers spread on his thighs. Antonia took the oil bottle and dripped some into the palm of her hand. Gideon's stomach muscles tightened as she looked at him. In its naked glory, his cock was bigger than she had realized. The thick length of it almost reached his navel. He was already wet, a pearl of moisture ready to slide down from his crown to coat his glistening shaft.

Antonia scooped up the wetness and sucked her finger into her mouth. His cock grew even bigger. She rubbed the oil between her palms and started to smooth it over the golden hair on his chest. His nipples hardened under her fingers. She paused to investigate them and the effect her fingers and mouth had on him. His pre-come soaked the front of her white shirt as she bent to her task.

Her nipples hardened even more as she knelt to slide oil across his shoulders and down his arms.

"You can rub harder than that. I won't break."

Gideon's husky request made her draw her nails across his skin. He shuddered and she did it again, reaching down to outline his buttocks with the rasp of her fingertips.

"Suck my cock."

She sat back and studied him. His hands remained on his thighs but they were fisted. His cock pumped with its own life as if begging for her touch.

"And should I be hard on you or soft?"

He swallowed, his throat working as he studied her through eyes hazed with passion. "Whichever you think I deserve."

She bent and licked her way around the swollen crown of his cock, concentrating on his taste and the sensation of his blood pumping against her skin. So stiff now that she feared he might break if she didn't give him release. She squeezed his shaft, thought about the glass rod buried inside her and clenched her own muscles. How would he feel inside her? As hard as the glass or simply bigger all over?

"Antonia..."

He slid a hand into her hair and guided her lips around his shaft. She drew him deep into her mouth, enjoying the wild raw smell of his passion. She felt a deep connection with his scent that went far beyond civilized words such as love and lust. From the first time he kissed her she had craved the taste of him, wanted to take him into herself and never let him go.

He flexed his hips, pushing his cock farther down her throat. She took him in greedily, sucking and pulling on his engorged flesh, her whole focus on pleasuring him and being pleasured in return. Her sex pulsed to the rhythm of her sucking and poured out cream to welcome him. She grabbed his buttocks, dug her nails in hard as he groaned low in his throat.

She almost snarled at him when he dragged her away and pressed her down into the pillows. His mouth settled over her pussy and she forgot to be angry. His clever tongue and slick fingers brought her to a level of excitement she hadn't believed possible. It was her turn to writhe as he pulled away from her just as she was about to climax.

He made her kneel again, her hands grasping the headboard, her legs apart. Her heart thudded in her chest as he removed the glass plug and nudged her with his cock.

"The last time someone fucked me, I was in my last term of school."

He penetrated her. She shook with the sensation of it as his wide cock slid inward helped by the oil. He paused to touch her nipples, squeezing the tips until it felt like a hot thin wire between pleasure and pain.

"One of the schoolmasters used to make us line up facing the fireplace and drop our breeches before he caned us." He rocked his hips, went deeper. "Sometimes he would deliberately delay our punishment. I can still remember the sensation of waiting, the cold air on my buttocks, the scratch of his quill pen as he attended to his work."

Antonia moaned as he caressed her swollen clit.

"When he made us wait, some of the boys shook and almost pissed themselves with fear. It aroused me. My cock would be hard. And when he finally got around to beating us it simply aroused me more. All that blood to the buttocks. We should try it some time."

"Did he not notice?"

She felt Gideon's smile even though she couldn't see his face. "Eventually. One evening he sent the other boys away and left me standing there with my breeches still down and my cock so hard it was dripping." She imagined him like that, felt her sex throb in response to the carnal image. "He brought his cane up and rubbed it over my cock until I had to clench my teeth against the ache."

She could scarcely breathe, so caught up in his words. "He told me that if I came, he would beat me again."

He surged forward until he was fully lodged inside her. She felt the hot press of his balls and furred stomach and the gentle rub of his fingers over her sex.

"Did you come?"

"Of course I did. He gave me six more strikes of the cane, wrapped his fingers around my cock and made me erect again."

He drew out of her until she feared he might not return. Her sex screamed with the need to come.

"He did that to me three more times until he finally fucked me."

He drove back inside her, shocking her anew with his huge size and width. She climaxed with a violence she had never experienced before. The pulses went on and on as he rocked back and forth against her and finally came himself. The hot wet heat of his seed spurted deep within her.

He kissed her neck, cradled her in his arms. "It was the most erotic experience of my life. Until now."

He slowly pulled out of her, leaving a trail of his hot come behind him.

Antonia collapsed onto the bed and he gathered her into his arms. His expression gentled as he kissed her mouth.

"I don't want to lose you, Antonia. Will you allow me to call on you tomorrow?"

She turned and smothered a smile against the pillows. Calling on her was tantamount to a declaration of marriage. She had been trying to work out how she might ask him to marry her and agree to her conditions. He'd just offered her the perfect opportunity.

Chapter Eight

ᔑᓍ

As Antonia walked demurely to the park with her aunt and cousin, she planned exactly what she intended to say to Gideon when he came to visit her. Even if he agreed to her suggestion of a marriage of convenience, she hoped he would still share her bed in a limited fashion. Her body still ached from his attentions and heated at the erotic thought of more sexual encounters. Last night he'd taught her about passion and about need.

A small part of her, a part she tried hard to ignore, wanted to experience the sensation of his cock sinking deep inside her sheath. Was she weakening toward him? If she allowed him to seduce her, she risked being trapped in a never-ending cycle of pregnancy and dependency like her mother before her. She shuddered at the thought.

Aunt Flora nudged her arm and guided her around a nursemaid pushing a baby carriage. "You seem a little distracted today, my love. Are you sure you are quite well?"

"I am in perfect health, dear Aunt, and happy to be out in this fresh spring air."

Flora frowned. "You should take care who hears you express such unhealthy views. Everyone knows that fresh air is extremely dangerous."

Antonia bit back a smile as her cousin Deborah ran up with a handful of daisies cupped in her palm. Her face was flushed, her bonnet askew.

"Oh, do help me pick some more, Antonia. We can make necklaces."

"Really, Deborah," Flora complained, "You are too old to make daisy chains and you will get your skirt and slippers muddy."

Ignoring Flora's comments, Antonia linked hands with Deb and headed for the grassy bank.

After completing several necklaces and bracelets to Deb's satisfaction, Antonia looked up to find her aunt in conversation with Gideon's father. She dusted off her skirt and went to join them. The viscount gave her an intimate smile which reminded her of Gideon at his most devious.

"Good morning, Miss Maxwell. I was just informing your aunt of the splendid impression you made on my son last night." He nodded jovially at Flora. "In fact, he actually came to see me this morning just to tell me how charming you were."

Antonia felt a blush steal over her cheeks. She hoped the viscount had no idea exactly how charming she had been to his son.

"Thank you, my lord. Lord Harcourt is an excellent dancer and a witty conversationalist."

The viscount nudged her with his cane. "And a fine-looking man, wouldn't you say? Your children would be both spirited and handsome."

She tried to look demure. "Your son didn't mention his desire for children, sir. We only had the one dance."

He drew her away from her aunt and began to walk along the daffodil-lined path, his expression sober. "Ah, but that's the main reason he wishes to marry so quickly, my dear. His chief desire is to safeguard the future of our illustrious family. He must have a son. Nothing is more important than that."

Antonia shivered as if the sun had passed behind a cloud. Something in the viscount's intense expression reminded her of her father. The viscount wanted an heir and he expected Gideon to provide him with one. Her vision of an uncomplicated future with Gideon crumbled in the dust. If he truly wanted an heir, no amount of money would make that up to him.

He patted her gloved hand. "I understand that my son intends to ask for your hand in marriage. I think he would make you a complacent husband." He lowered his voice. "And may I suggest you ignore any rumors which suggest that Gideon's first wife killed herself because she couldn't bear to carry his child? That woman was mentally unstable and extremely selfish. She would have done anything to deprive him of a son."

She concentrated on walking and pulling air into her suddenly constricted lungs. It seemed that in her panicked rush to decide her own future she'd chosen to ignore the truth. Gideon sounded just as ruthless as her father. Had he driven his pregnant wife to kill herself because he didn't consider her a fit mother for his all important heir? She realized the viscount was still speaking and automatically held out her hand as he made his adieus.

The springlike beauty of the park held no more appeal for her. She had to prevent Gideon from meeting with her cousin to ask for her hand in marriage. She could no longer put off asking him about his wife's death either. Depending on his response, she could decide whether to propose her marriage bargain to him or run back to Wales as fast as she could. She stopped dead in the center of the path as the sensation of being trapped intensified. It was imperative to write him a note telling him not to call on her cousin and to ask him to meet her at Madame Desiree's that night instead.

Turning to her aunt, she pressed her trembling hand to her brow. "I think you are right. All this fresh air is giving me a headache. Can we go home?"

There was a distinctly different feel to the atmosphere at Madame Desiree's on a Tuesday night. Only a few of the massive candelabras were lit, leaving most of the rooms in a deep shadowy gloom. As Antonia progressed up the stairs, she noticed most of the clientele were men. As a result the place felt darker and less welcoming. There was no sign of Madame Desiree.

She waited in the main salon having sent a servant to ascertain Gideon's whereabouts. A group of rowdy young men entered the salon, two women in their midst. The women were dressed in loud, clashing garments which reminded her of the brothel Gideon had taken her to rather than the sleek elegance she normally associated with Madame Desiree's.

Their shrieking and high-pitched giggling began to grate on her already highly strung nerves. She moved away from the fireplace and headed for the opposite end of the room. As she passed by, one of the women sank onto a couch and opened her legs in coarse invitation.

"Ooh, pretty boy, come and spend some time with me."

Antonia ignored the offer and concentrated her attention on the door. Another man fell on top of the woman and moved his hips in crude, urgent thrusts, roared on by the encouragement of the young bucks. Antonia strode toward the door. She would wait for Gideon in the hall downstairs.

A hand grasped her elbow. She tried to shake it off until she realized it was Peter Howard.

"Mr. Smith. What are you doing here?"

Antonia felt herself blush. The last time she'd seen Peter he'd been naked, his tongue flicking between her legs as he made her come.

"I was supposed to meet Gideon. Is he here?"

"He's upstairs." Peter pulled her into the corridor. "Are you sure he told you to come here tonight?" He glanced at the tangle of skirts and breeches in the salon. "Tuesdays are usually for men only."

Before she could reply, a shriek from the woman at the bottom of the pile of bodies on the couch drew her attention back to the main salon. The woman fell to the floor and lost her wig to reveal short cropped hair. She giggled and kicked her legs in the air, dislodging her petticoats to display hairy legs and the unmistakable sight of an aroused male member. Antonia studied the strange sight until she abruptly looked away. Peter continued to stare at her a faint smile on his lips.

"That woman is a man!" she hissed.

He smiled. "That is why I am surprised Gideon agreed to meet you here. This is Madame Desiree's attempt to recreate a Molly house where gentleman of a particular persuasion can dress up as women and find other gentlemen who appreciate them. As I said, it's not a suitable place for a lady. Come along, I'll take you to him."

Antonia followed Peter up yet another flight of stairs, trying to ignore the increasing number of men dressed up as women. An awful thought struck her as Peter knocked on one of the doors. Did Gideon dress up too?

She let out a breath as she spied him sitting at a card table, dressed with his usual care in a brown coat, cream waistcoat and buff breeches. He acknowledged her with a quick nod and returned to his game. One of the other players had a "woman" sitting on his knee. His hand was hidden beneath her pink taffeta skirt.

She took the opportunity to study the false woman beneath her lowered lashes. Even the obscene amount of badly applied face paint couldn't quite disguise the shadow of the man's beard. Why would any man want to kiss someone like that?

Antonia allowed Peter to bring her a glass of wine as she waited for Gideon to finish his game. Despite the strangeness of her surroundings, the lull gave her a chance to work on her speech to Gideon.

Eventually, he got up and strolled toward her. After a cheerful wave, Peter took his place at the table. Gideon bowed. "Is there something wrong?"

His tone was cool, his face a bland mask. A frisson of fear laced with rage settled uneasily in her belly. "I sent you a note."

He raised an eyebrow. "I received it. I wrongly assumed that you asked me not to visit your cousin because you were ill." His gaze swept her from head to toe. "That does not appear to be the case."

"Can we talk privately?"

He studied her for a long moment. "If that is what you wish." He gestured at one of the "women". "Are you sure that you don't want to stay here and dress up for me? It might be amusing."

She took a step closer until she had to look up into his face. Anger shook through her in juddering waves. "Why? Would it make it easier for you to fuck me and get me with child if you thought I was a man dressed up as a woman?"

His expression hardened. "What in God's name are you talking about?"

He led her out of the room and into one of the vacant ones opposite. Antonia shut the door firmly behind her and studied him.

"I can't marry you, Gideon."

He raised one eyebrow. "I don't believe I've asked you to."

She balled her hands into fists. "That's why I told you not to call today. I had to speak to you before you spoke to my cousin."

He walked across to the fireplace and paused in front of it. "What exactly did you want to say to me?"

Her fingers itched to slap the faint trace of amusement from his face. "Is it true that your wife was pregnant when she died?"

His expression sharpened. "Yes. Who told you that?"

"It's common knowledge."

He watched her, one arm resting on the mantelpiece. "So?"

She gathered the shreds of her composure. "My mother was pregnant when she killed herself. She endured ten pregnancies because my father wanted a male heir."

"Ah, you think I am like your father."

"You seem to share his sexual tastes." She took a deep breath. "I thought to propose a bargain to you but it seems I was misinformed. I refuse to be used to breed a new dynasty of Harcourts with another man who hates to make love to a woman."

"What makes you think that?"

"I saw you, Gideon. I saw you with Peter. You *wanted* me to see you."

"For God's sake, I wanted you to see what—" He took a step toward her, his eyes blazing with a cold, icy fire. She held out a hand as if she could ward him off and he stopped.

"I see it now. After you saw me with Peter, you thought you could persuade me to marry you and then leave you alone, didn't you? Did you let me inside you to gain my trust?" His mouth curved into a dismissive smile. "You never wanted a real sexual relationship with a man, did you?"

He moved back and leaned against the mantelpiece to study her. "Of course, in exchange for your silence about my male lovers I'd get another wife who despised me and refused me her bed." Gideon began to laugh, the sound harsh. "You are just like Caroline. Blackmail is never pretty whatever you choose to call it."

"That's not true!"

His answering sneer was unmistakable. Antonia strode up to him and slapped his face. When she tried to repeat the action, his hand shot out and caught her wrist.

Her voice shook with the effort not to cry. "I'm going home now. I won't be back."

"Run away then, little man."

He kissed her, his tongue probing between her lips in an intimate and possessive exploration. She forced herself to pull away before she succumbed to the desperate need to kiss him back.

He brushed her swollen lower lip with the tip of his finger. "What's upsetting you most, Antonia, the fact that I won't agree to your plans or the fact that you still want me anyway?"

Without another word, she ran for the door, leaving him alone in the center of the room.

Gideon touched his bruised cheek as the door slammed behind Antonia. Strange how his life seemed to be repeating itself. He poured himself a large glass of brandy amazed that his fingers were still steady. Caroline had blackmailed him into staying married to her after threatening to expose his penchant for male lovers. In return for her silence he'd been forced to watch her fornicate her way through the *ton* and every rough working man she could get her hands on.

He wasn't prepared to make such a bargain again. He took a cigar out of his case and lit it, allowing the smoke to soothe his nerves. Antonia was an incredibly passionate woman. Did she really believe she'd be content in a marriage without proper sex? If he married her under those circumstances he could guarantee she would be looking for a lover within a month.

He blew out a smoke ring. And how had she become to believe that he only slept with men? She must know in her heart that he was more than capable of satisfying a woman. God, yesterday she'd trusted him enough to let him fuck her arse...

He tossed back half of the brandy. What the hell had he been thinking? To fall in love with a woman after an acquaintance of only a few weeks? His half-emptied glass glinted in the candlelight. He threw it in the fireplace where it smashed into ice-sharp splinters. Better to drink from the bottle anyway. A black urge to seek oblivion in the alcohol burned in his gut.

Someone knocked on the door. He glanced up as Peter came in.

"Forgive me if I am interfering, but I escorted young Anthony into a hackney cab."

Gideon tipped the ash from his cigar onto the carpet. "Thank you. I would've done it myself but she was too angry with me."

Peter came and sat opposite him, avoiding the shards of glass as best he could. "All is not well in love's fair bower, I assume?"

"As far as I understand it, she thinks I prefer men but she still wants me to marry her so that she doesn't have to have sex and ever get pregnant."

"Ah, that certainly complicates things." Peter studied the fire and then the toe of his boot. "Why on earth did you think it would be a good idea to let her see you fucking me?"

"Dammit, I wanted to show her that my sexual tastes were unusual. I wanted to see if she would accept me as I am before I asked her to marry me." Gideon ran an agitated hand through his hair. "Why do women make things so complicated? I've done everything but fuck her because I promised not to take her virginity, although she seems to have conveniently forgotten that."

He glanced up sharply as Peter concealed a smile. "You think this is amusing?"

"No, of course not. It's damned complicated but I admit it is a little entertaining to see you caught in the throes of passion and unrequited love."

Gideon frowned. Did he love her? He'd already admitted as much earlier. The thought of losing her made him feel cold to the marrow and fiercely possessive. To his surprise, despite her behavior, she still represented everything he yearned for in a mate.

"She tried to blackmail me just like Caroline did."

Peter raised an eyebrow. "She is no Caroline. She is not used to dissembling. I suspect she is merely trying to make the best of an impossible situation."

Gideon thought about the hell Antonia's parents had lived through and the effect on their child. Did she truly believe all men were monsters? Had fear pushed her to reject him? The brandy curdled in his stomach.

"Exactly why did she walk out on you?"

"That's what puzzles me," Gideon said. "After last night, I thought we had reached an understanding. Now she seems determined to believe that I am exactly like her father and intend to keep her pregnant for the rest of her life."

Peter laughed. "She sounds as if she's been talking to *your* father."

Gideon stubbed out his cigar. "Hell and damnation! I told him I was intending to propose to her. Do you think he paid her a visit?"

"It would be just like him to try and prepare the bride for her future role as the mother of another generation of the glorious Harcourt family."

Gideon downed the rest of his brandy. "Then perhaps it is up to me to make that role clear to her."

Chapter Nine
සා

Antonia closed the door of her bedchamber and leaned against it. Her cousin had decided to host a dinner party for all her potential suitors and their families. She had spent the whole evening being gazed upon by various mamas and other interested family members without any attempt to hide their interest in the size of her inheritance and her general state of health.

At one point, Antonia had wondered if Charles intended to make her stand on the dining room table, call the room to order and start the auction. She was still surprised no one had asked to see her teeth.

She closed her eyes. It was impossible. She couldn't marry any of them. Gideon was the only man who had appeared to understand her and even that had been a sham. Tomorrow she would pack her bags and return to Wales and the sanctuary of her home. It was unlikely that anyone would come after her for a while. A hot trickle of tears stung her cheeks. At least she'd experienced some joy in London even if it had come to naught.

"Don't cry."

She opened her eyes, simultaneously aware that her bedroom window was open and that Gideon sat at his ease by her fireplace.

"What in God's name are you doing here?"

He shrugged. "I thought it was time we continued our conversation."

She glanced wildly at the door. "You have to leave. If anyone sees you, my reputation will be in ruins." She clutched at her hair. "Is that what you want? Are you trying to force me into marriage?"

A slight frown appeared on his forehead. "Your willingness to believe the worst of me is becoming annoying." His smile was not pleasant. "But, you do have a point. If you scream and bring the household down on us, I'll not leave."

He got up and walked past her to the door. He locked it and pocketed the key. "Now perhaps we can start again."

Antonia watched in horror as he shrugged out of his black coat and silver waistcoat. Despite her best efforts her body gave a little leap of excitement. "What are you doing?"

He glanced at her as he removed his cravat and cuff links. "I'm undressing."

"Why?"

"Because I wish to be naked when I make love to you."

She folded her arms tightly over her chest. "You don't have anything to prove, my lord. I thought I'd made it clear that I refuse to give myself to a man who just wants heirs."

His fingers worked the buttons of his breeches. He was already aroused. He wrapped a hand around his cock and stroked himself. "Ah but you are forgetting something. You already have my word that I will not seduce you."

He worked off his boots and pulled his shirt over his head to reveal his muscled chest. Antonia felt her sex pulse in response. "Are you saying that the only reason you haven't made love to me is because you gave me your word that you wouldn't?"

His mouth tightened into a thin determined line. "My word is never given lightly. If you wish me to fuck you properly, then you will have to give me leave."

Antonia stared at him. Her throat constricted as she tried to force the words out. "I can't."

His fingers stilled on his breeches. "You do not desire me?"

Kate Pearce

Her gaze swept the magnificence of his body and she shivered. He was so male, so threatening, so... "Gideon, I can't. I'm too afraid."

"Afraid I'll hurt you?"

"No, that I'll get pregnant."

He sat down on the side of her bed, watching her intently. "I'm quite prepared to give up my male lovers if that is what you want. I'm not your father, Antonia, I don't hate women."

She faced him, hands clenched together at her waist. "And I'm not your wife."

He sighed. "I was wrong to assume you wished to blackmail me into marriage."

Antonia gulped in shock. "That's not what I meant at all. I thought I could bargain my fortune against a promise not to force me into bed."

"I don't want your money." He buttoned his breeches, his expression bleak. "Do you really believe any fool who agreed to such a ridiculous bargain would keep his word? On marriage a woman becomes her husband's property. Legally there is no such thing as rape within marriage. I can guarantee you would've been pregnant within a year." He looked up at her. "Despite what you imagine, money cannot always buy you what you want."

"That's why I have decided to return to Wales."

"You can't run away from everything, Antonia."

She took a step toward him and then another until she stood over him. He held her gaze.

"Release me from my vow, let me make love to you and then decide if you wish to leave."

She studied him suspiciously. "And if I decided to go, you would let me?"

"Of course."

"You are very arrogant, Gideon."

"I am very good in bed."

214

She twisted her fingers together until he reached out and covered her hands with his own. "What is it, love?"

"Gideon, I can't." She knew she must sound like a bleating goat.

"When do you bleed?"

"Why should I tell you?"

He drew in a deep breath as if seeking patience. "Because the closer you are to your monthly cycle, the less likely you are to get pregnant."

"You are only saying that so you can bed me." Dammit, her voice was shaking again.

He reached up and tucked a lock of her hair behind her ear. "I'm telling you the truth. And if you are still fearful of conceiving, I have other methods to prevent pregnancy." He smiled. "I also bring with me an invitation from Madame Desiree to visit and discuss the many ways a woman can avoid bearing a child."

"You don't want a nursery full of children?"

"You *have* been talking to my father, haven't you? He has other children and the chance to have many heirs. I told him to keep his foolish dynastic ambitions to himself."

"But isn't it sinful to prevent conception?"

"That is a matter between you and your conscience, Antonia. Never think I would judge you for that."

She stared at him, her breathing erratic, unable to deny the need coursing through her at the sight of him half undressed, sitting at his ease on her bed. It was imperative that she kept her anger alive before she gave into an unheard of urge to weep on his chest. She dug her fingernails into her palms.

"I thought this was just a game. Something to amuse you."

"Perhaps at first it was." He shrugged, the gesture fluid. "I soon realized that you were an exceptional woman."

"Yet you still managed to keep from fucking me."

He frowned. "We agreed that I would teach you about pleasure. And as I've already said, you made me promise not to seduce you. I kept my word."

Was he saying that he had wanted her as a woman from the first? Had she deliberately misread his intention to keep his promise as a lack of desire? He picked up his coat, took something out of the pocket and laid it on the bed. For a terrible moment, she thought he planned to leave her money.

"If I'd had more time with you, I intended to introduce you to this method of ensuring a man doesn't pick up the French pox."

Antonia studied the thin envelope which seemed to be made of some kind of filmy animal skin. "Is it snake skin?"

Gideon opened the envelope and withdrew another piece of the thin parchment-like material. This longer, narrower piece had ribbons around the open end and was sewn shut at the bottom. He carefully slid one finger inside and held it up.

"It's pig intestine. The same thing used to make sausage skin."

She glanced down at his groin before she could stop herself. "It goes over your cock?"

"That is correct. Not only does it prevent disease, but it means that a man's seed remains trapped inside it after he comes which seems to prevent pregnancy."

Antonia touched the wrinkled cream skin with her fingertip. She imagined it might feel as if you wore a glove.

"Do you use these?"

"Of course I do."

"Did you use them with your wife?"

A muscle twitched in his cheek. "My wife refused to allow me to use them, which is why I eventually refused to have sex with her."

"But the baby she carried…"

"Wasn't mine. She had no idea who it belonged to either, although she rather believed it was one of the stable boys at Madame Desiree's."

She stared at him, noted the lines of strain on his face. Had he ever discussed this before or had he simply ignored the gossip and allowed his reputation to be damaged beyond repair? The house seemed unusually quiet around her, as if everything was holding its breath.

"Did you threaten to expose her? Is that why she killed herself?"

"On the contrary, I offered to bring the child up as my own." He smiled, although it was obviously an effort. "For me, her pregnancy was a blessing. The succession would be assured and I wouldn't have to go near her bed again." He looked away from her. "Unfortunately, my wife decided she would rather die than live in my debt. Her words, not mine."

He laid the delicate sheath back on the counterpane. He sounded tired. "There are other methods to prevent pregnancy as I'm sure Madame Desiree will tell you."

Her throat tightened as he reclaimed his shirt and boots and began to dress.

"I thought you intended to make love to me."

He paused as he arranged his cravat and pinned it in place. "I've changed my mind. I'm not a monster, Antonia. Your fear of pregnancy is understandable. Perhaps simply showing you that it is avoidable is not enough to calm your concerns."

"That is very generous of you. So having ruined me for any other man you now intend to walk away from me as well?"

He buttoned his waistcoat. "Ah, but you see, unlike most men, I'm trying to be honest with you. You are right. The only way to avoid being pregnant is never to make love to anyone."

She forced herself to speak through the tight bands constricting her throat. "Are you suggesting I am a coward?"

He shrugged into his coat and settled it over his broad shoulders. "I've realized that allowing someone to make love to you requires trust. And trust has to go both ways." He turned to face her. "I would do everything in my power to stop you getting pregnant, but I might not succeed. Would you turn on me then and hate me as your mother hated your father?"

He held her gaze, his blue eyes steady. "If we conceived a child together, I would welcome it without reservation. But I'm not prepared to stand by and watch another woman kill herself rather than carry a child."

He kissed her forehead and handed her back the key. "I love you, Antonia but I fear even that is not enough." He walked toward the window, leaving her by the bed. She bit her lip as he disappeared over the sill and faded into the blackness.

She gazed at the faint indentation on her bedcovers and the sheath he had left there. Was he right? Was she too afraid to ever trust anyone with her love and her body? She sank to her knees and started to sob. The sound almost a keening for something lost beyond recall.

Gideon had understood her to the last. He'd ripped apart all her illusions about what she wanted and shown her the frightened girl who still watched helplessly as her mother walked into the lake and drowned.

And now she was alone with that memory and the horrible sensation that she had just lost more than she would ever know.

Chapter Ten

∞

In the soft dawn light, the lake looked peaceful and untouched. A group of ancient willow trees bent over the water like maidens washing their long hair. Blackbirds sang challenges to neighbors and larks swooped overhead to greet the new day. Antonia sat on the bank and hugged her knees to her chest. There were no ghosts here. No sense of her mother and the frightened girl she had been. She closed her eyes and tried to picture her mother's expression as she slid beneath the water. Calmness and acceptance. As if she had finally found peace.

Her home was as tranquil and welcoming as ever but it was no longer her refuge. It hadn't taken her long to realize that meeting Gideon had changed her too much to ever allow her to return to her old life. He'd understood that she trusted him long before she had admitted it. After understanding that, it was but a short step to acknowledging that she was wrong to run away from him.

Antonia couldn't imagine giving up like her mother had. She stared at a pair of swans as they waddled up to the edge of the lake, awkward on land but transformed after their first smooth glide into the water. Swans mated for life. Was it possible for people to do the same?

A month in the tranquil countryside at her home on the Gower had brought her to this place and this decision. If she had any chance to redeem her life, it had to be now. She couldn't change the past but she was no longer prepared to let it ruin her future. She tensed as a horse neighed close by. The soft sound of booted feet on the cobblestone path behind her made her close her eyes.

"Am I welcome, then?"

She opened her eyes to stare up at Gideon. He looked tired, purple shadows under his eyes and a day's growth of golden beard on his jaw. His boots were muddy and his cloak splashed with dirt. She'd only sent the letter a week ago. He must have ridden like the devil to get to her so quickly.

"Of course you are welcome."

He came down on one knee, a posy of wildflowers in his hand. His thick cloak billowed out around him in the soft breeze as he laid the flowers at her feet. Dappled light through the willow trees gave his face an intensity she found hard to ignore.

"I'm still afraid, Gideon."

He smiled and took her hands in his. "So am I." He glanced around the secluded lake and laid his cloak on the ground. "I think this is the perfect spot, don't you?"

She swallowed as he leaned forward and kissed her, his mouth warm and full of promises. She opened to him, let him explore, possess and enchant her with his scent and taste. With a groan he deepened the kiss and drew her into his arms.

His hands encircled her waist until she was pressed against him from shoulder to knee. She could feel his erection hot and hard through the thin muslin of her gown and petticoats. He kissed her throat, slid her bodice sleeves down her arms and caressed her breasts.

"You have no corset on. Were you expecting someone?"

She smiled at his quizzical expression. "I rarely wear a corset in the country." She glanced down at her small breasts cupped in his hands. "It's not as if I need one."

His mouth surrounded her right breast, concentrating on her nipple as he sucked and molded her flesh. God, she had missed him so much. In a hurry now she helped him out of his garments until only his breeches remained. She was also bared to the waist, her skimpy dress pushed down, her nipples hard and rosy from his mouth and fingers.

She stroked his chest, ran her fingers down his back until he shivered and kissed her again. A wave of intense longing engulfed her as he slid a hand up her thigh and pressed against the heat of her sex. She opened her legs gladly for him. Whimpered as he stroked her and slid his fingers inside.

"When do you bleed?"

His fingers kept up their rocking motion and made it hard for her to speak. "In two days." His growl of satisfaction reverberated against her mouth, blocking further words.

He laid her down on his cloak and knelt between her thighs, pushing them wide so that her pussy was completely exposed to his heated gaze. He flicked her swollen bud with his finger. "I've missed you. I've missed this."

She groaned as he hooked her thighs over his shoulders and licked her sex with long, greedy laps, his tongue rough and demanding on her already aroused flesh. Her cream flowed to join the wetness of his tongue until the smell of her arousal rose around them. She dug her nails into his arms as she spiraled toward a climax.

As she came, he thrust his fingers back inside her, worked them deeper and wider as his mouth still pleasured her. She felt overwhelmed with desire, desperate for every new sensation he gave her. She cried out when she came again, mindlessly pushing her hips forward, grinding her sex into his face.

When she stopped trembling, he sat back on his heels, his face wet with her cream. His breeches bulged at the front as his cock pressed against the buckskin. Slowly she reached up and ran her finger down the length of his shaft. His pupils dilated until his eyes looked almost black.

He licked his lips and followed the movement of her fingers over his cock. What would he do if she changed her mind again and was truly too terrified to take him inside her? He tried to ignore the urgent press of his flesh and the need to possess her. Her letter had said only that she had changed her mind and wanted to stop being a coward. Was she strong enough to go through with it?

Did it matter?

A sense of peace flooded through him as he looked down at her.

"You don't have to do this, Antonia. We can make love in other ways." He realized he meant it. "I'd rather have you as my wife than any other woman. And if that means keeping to your bargain, I will agree."

He thought about never having sex again. Never having a child. It no longer seemed important. He loved her and intended to be faithful.

She smiled up at him, her expression thoughtful. "If I deny you my bed, will you simply fill my place with a man?"

"If you become my wife, why would I ever need to do that?"

She brushed the corner of his mouth with her fingertip. "But I would be forcing you to deny a part of yourself that I find particularly intriguing."

He struggled to keep some blood in his brain as the rest deserted him for his cock. "You would allow me to bed men?"

"Only if you allowed me to watch."

Gideon closed his eyes as Antonia flattened her fingers over his shaft.

Damnation, he wanted to move his hips, seek the pressure of her touch. He gritted his teeth against the ache in his balls and stiff cock. With a cry of exasperation, she ripped at the buttons of his breeches and he yelped.

"Gideon, it's very sweet of you to be so noble but I want you. I want you now while my courage lasts." She sighed as his cock emerged from the ripped top of his breeches.

He let out a breath he hadn't realized he was holding. "Are you sure?"

"I refuse to live in the past. I don't want to end up like my mother, too scared to face the future and too desperate to change it."

He stripped off his breeches and boots and knelt naked between her thighs. His hands trembled as he carefully slid the French letter over his cock and tightened the ribbons. His shaft jerked as Antonia stroked him.

Grasping his cock in one hand, he positioned himself close to her wet and welcoming sex. Damn, he felt like a virgin himself. He stared into her eyes and saw there only open invitation and shy desire. He slid in until the crown of his cock met the resistance of her maidenhead.

He wanted to thrust and make her his completely but he held back, kissing her mouth, fondling her swollen clit until she started to convulse around him. Catching a hand in her hair, he held her passion-filled gaze.

"This is your last chance to say me nay. I will try and pull out if I can, but sometimes it's difficult." She didn't respond, all her attention on his shaft. "It might hurt for a moment, trust me."

He pressed forward, past the thin barrier until he was sheathed inside her. She lay quiet beneath him, her muscles rigid. Her nails dug into his back.

"Are you all right?"

Would she panic now the deed was done? Would she follow her mother into the loneliness and silence of the lake?

She slowly opened her dove-gray eyes. It was like looking into paradise.

"Don't stop," she whispered.

His throat tightened as he began to move slowly within her. He watched her face, waiting for her to lose herself in her passion again. She brought her legs up around his hips and planted her heels in his buttocks, holding him deep with her. It was enough to make him buck against her, driving her forward now, commanding her body to release its secrets to him and him alone.

She cried out, the sound muffled by the urgent press of his mouth and he felt his balls tighten, ready to come. With all his strength, he reached down between their bodies and made sure the sheath was still tightly fitted to his cock before he allowed himself to let go.

A flood of pleasure shuddered through him as he came so hard he thought the top of his cock might explode. He remembered to pull out and groped for the French letter to make sure it hadn't split. With a rugged sigh, he rolled onto his back and brought Antonia with him. She fitted against his chest, her head tucked under his chin as if she belonged there.

"Will you marry me, Antonia?"

She kissed his shoulder. "Yes, if you will have me, although you should know that my cousin might refuse me my inheritance if he doesn't approve of you as a potential husband."

Gideon smiled. "His approval only matters if it matters to you, my love. Otherwise we can tell him to go hang himself. I don't need your money and I promise to allow you to spend all of mine."

He settled her more comfortably in his arms, admired the way the light stippled her rosy skin. "I'm glad you've decided to marry me, because I have already made plans for our wedding night. After we've consummated our love in our marriage bed, I'm taking you out to a cockfight."

She reared up on one elbow and regarded him. "In my gentleman's attire, I assume?"

"Naturally. And on our way home, I intend to coax you up against a wall and show you a real fighting cock."

Her eyes widened and she stroked his shoulder. "Gideon, you are full of surprises."

He sighed. "No, my dear, you are. I never thought I would find a woman I would feel comfortable with. Or who would put up with my peculiar tendencies."

"I love you, Gideon. Just as you are because you love me."

He held her gaze. "And that is truly the best gift of all, isn't it?" He remembered his first sight of her face, swathed in another woman's silk stocking, the humor and courage behind her bold stare. He kissed her swollen mouth and glanced up at the sky to judge the time. They still had a while before anyone would come looking for them. His cock thickened against her belly and he sat up.

"I have several more French letters in my pocket. It seems a shame to waste them."

Antonia rolled off him and went to investigate his coat pockets. He came up behind her and guided her forward onto her hands and knees. His hands cupped her breasts as his shaft rubbed against the small of her back. His lovemaking was as wonderful as she had imagined it would be. Her fears receded into the distance. He kissed her neck and she shivered.

Life was for living. Her decision to trust Gideon was too fragile and uncertain not to worry her a little. She glanced at the lake, knew her life would never be so calm and flat again. Gideon would love her in any way she wanted and they would face the future together. His warm hand slid down to her mound and settled over her sex. She arched her back in welcome.

In some ways it felt as if her life had just begun.

Why an electronic book?

We live in the Information Age—an exciting time in the history of human civilization, in which technology rules supreme and continues to progress in leaps and bounds every minute of every day. For a multitude of reasons, more and more avid literary fans are opting to purchase e-books instead of paper books. The question from those not yet initiated into the world of electronic reading is simply: *Why?*

1. *Price.* An electronic title at Ellora's Cave Publishing and Cerridwen Press runs anywhere from 40% to 75% less than the cover price of the exact same title in paperback format. Why? Basic mathematics and cost. It is less expensive to publish an e-book (no paper and printing, no warehousing and shipping) than it is to publish a paperback, so the savings are passed along to the consumer.

2. *Space.* Running out of room in your house for your books? That is one worry you will never have with electronic books. For a low one-time cost, you can purchase a handheld device specifically designed for e-reading. Many e-readers have large, convenient screens for viewing. Better yet, hundreds of titles can be stored within your new library—on a single microchip. There are a variety of e-readers from different manufacturers. You can also read e-books on your PC or laptop computer. (Please note that Ellora's Cave does not endorse any specific brands.

You can check our websites at www.ellorascave.com or www.cerridwenpress.com for information we make available to new consumers.)

3. *Mobility.* Because your new e-library consists of only a microchip within a small, easily transportable e-reader, your entire cache of books can be taken with you wherever you go.

4. *Personal Viewing Preferences.* Are the words you are currently reading too small? Too large? Too... ANNOYING? Paperback books cannot be modified according to personal preferences, but e-books can.

5. *Instant Gratification.* Is it the middle of the night and all the bookstores near you are closed? Are you tired of waiting days, sometimes weeks, for bookstores to ship the novels you bought? Ellora's Cave Publishing sells instantaneous downloads twenty-four hours a day, seven days a week, every day of the year. Our webstore is never closed. Our e-book delivery system is 100% automated, meaning your order is filled as soon as you pay for it.

Those are a few of the top reasons why electronic books are replacing paperbacks for many avid readers.

As always, Ellora's Cave and Cerridwen Press welcome your questions and comments. We invite you to email us at Comments@ellorascave.com or write to us directly at Ellora's Cave Publishing Inc., 1056 Home Avenue, Akron, OH 44310-3502.

COMING TO A BOOKSTORE NEAR YOU!

ELLORA'S CAVE

Bestselling Authors Tour

UPDATES AVAILABLE AT
WWW.ELLORASCAVE.COM

errídwen, the Celtic Goddess of wisdom, was the muse who brought inspiration to storytellers and those in the creative arts. Cerridwen Press encompasses the best and most innovative stories in all genres of today's fiction. Visit our site and discover the newest titles by talented authors who still get inspired - much like the ancient storytellers did, once upon a time.

Cerrídwen Press
www.cerrídwenpress.com

Discover for yourself why readers can't get enough
of the multiple award-winning publisher
Ellora's Cave.

Whether you prefer e-books or paperbacks,

be sure to visit EC on the web at
www.ellorascave.com

for an erotic reading experience that will leave you
breathless.